736 Dominion
Isn't There Anymore

736 Dominion Isn't There Anymore

Allan Royal

Inglewood
PRESS

Front cover photograph and design, courtesy Allan Royal
Back cover photograph © Nicholas Alan, 2019

Book design by Alex Bolduc

ISBN 978-0-9949861-9-1

This is a work of fiction. Names, characters, places and incidents either are the product of the author's imagination or are used fictionally. The author's use of names of historical figures, places or events is not intended to change the fictional character of the work. In all other respects, any resemblance to persons living or dead is entirely coincidental.

All photographs have been provided by the author, with appropriate permissions.

INGLEWOOD PRESS
180 Bloor Street West, Suite 1200
Toronto M5S 2V6, Canada
www.inglewoodpress.ca

PRINTED IN CANADA BY COACH HOUSE PRESS

for Mum

Introduction

ALLAN ROYAL is admired in the theatre world throughout Canada. His request that I write an introduction to this book occasioned a wry chuckle followed by a sobering question: how well, really, do I know Allan Royal? More seriously, it begged larger questions which I believe rest at the heart of his stories: how well, really, do we know any of those whom we love, who have loved us in return and who have shaped our Being? How well can we ever know ourselves, except in relation to those others?

I have known and loved Allan, and been known and loved by him, as a friend and colleague for over four decades. When first we met, I was a starry-eyed young actress in the true sense of the cliché, an apprentice in the acting company at Toronto's St. Lawrence Centre. Allan was a recognized, accomplished actor … charming, gifted, enigmatic. And he scared the living daylights out of me. One day after rehearsal, to my amazement, he offered me a ride home. Once in the car he said, "Hey, I know a place where they make the best coffee in the city. Why don't we stop in and have a cup before I drop you off?"

As I intuited, that place was Allan's apartment. I pointedly reminded him I was newly married. It turned out that Allan did make the best coffee in Toronto, which came with a surprising side of insight and compassion about who I was and what might lie ahead for me. I might have considered him presumptuous had he not been so inexplicably caring … and on the mark.

Within a few years my marriage ended. Allan was by then living with my best friend. They took me in, and fate found me more or less in Allan's care. Every morning I traipsed upstairs and sat weeping at the kitchen table while he made me coffee; strong, rich Medaglia d'Oro. Honest to goodness, those mornings saved my life. There have since been other kitchen tables, many coffee shops and bookstores where I have sat with Allan and shared an ever-deepening discourse about our lives and work, which, for both of us, included a desire and a compulsion to write.

Allan comes from a lost world, as do all of us who are granted the gift of age. His world was one of big brothers, best buddies and maple-baked beans. It was a world of snow-crusted cement stoops, steamies and poutine, the magic and mystery of fulsome girls who wore peter-pan collars and Tabu perfume. It was also a crucible in which French and English cultures cleaved and clashed beneath his own roof. His schooling in the harsh discipline of what was then Quebec Catholicism was pitched against a rough but tender spirituality fostered in the streets of the post-war, industrial neighbourhood where he became a man. He was marked by an exquisite tension between his intense love for that world and his driving need to grow beyond its boundaries.

When Allan left Montreal to make his way in the world, he took with him the faith of family and friends. He took the traits so often imposed on and developed by the youngest sibling, those of patience and keen observance. He took with him the knowledge not just of love's thrill but also its cost, and therefore its true value. Everything that flows from Allan flows from love. His humanity, and therefore his art, is grounded in it, whether he is playing Shakespeare's fiery Tybalt, a farcical Italian waiter, a man stranded and fighting to stay alive in the far north, or an ironic crime reporter; whether he is writing a story, renovating a house or building a friendship. He is able to see clear through to the heart of a person – what they're ashamed or afraid of, and yet what they're trying so hard to bring into the world.

What do I know about Allan Royal? I know he is a witness-bearer, an ethnographer of Life, an astute judge of character. I know that he is fair and loyal and hard working. He is a father, a grandfather and a devoted husband who is, rightly, absolutely smitten by his wife (as are all who know her). I know he has magic blue eyes, and sees magic in much of what he beholds. He's a skilled carpenter, an unparalleled baker tourtière, and a true lover of women. He is a risk-taker and a master of improvisation learned at the hand of George Luscombe at Toronto Workshop Theatre. He is a listener with an ear for Shakespeare, for the music of the French language, for the rhythms of Quebecois dialect and for his favourite poet, Robert Service. He's an antic performer who can be so funny I've thought I might die laughing. For me, Allan's stories are not unlike Grandma Moses' paintings in their seeming simplicity and sometimes quirky rendering, but they are no less profound in their revelations of what it means to be human. They are, in fact, piercing testimony about how to wake up every morning and love the world all over again when your heart (whether young or old) has suffered a terrible growing pain the night before, and dawn brings the hollow knowledge that nothing will ever be the same.

In writing, as in friendship, Allan offers what he knows about the love that shaped him in the giving and taking. He takes this knowledge and weaves it into fiction that seems so real you feel it happened to you. Consider these stories an invitation. Pour yourself a cup of strong, hot coffee, settle down, and spend some time with Allan Royal. You may learn things about yourself you never knew....

— Heather Summerhayes Cariou

The Thinking-Man's Game

IT WAS EARLY MAY and the cool morning air came in through the window and passed over my body. I was awake. I had been lying there in my pajamas, nice and warm beneath the covers, for at least fifteen minutes. I knew I had to get up, so I threw the covers off and tried not to let my bare feet touch the cold wood floor. I quickly jumped into my slippers. My bed was tucked under the window in the corner of the bedroom I shared with my brother. Frankie was already up and eating breakfast. I hurried down the hallway toward the kitchen. I could hear him talking to my mother, his voice loud and complaining.

"But, I got stuff to do today! Why can't it be next Saturday?"

When I reached the kitchen, the first thing my mother said was, "Go run the water and get into the bath!" There wasn't a hello or a good morning. Being the youngest is always a burden.

I was faced with Frankie stuffing his face with banana pancakes covered with maple syrup and butter. A large, half-full glass of cold milk sat on the table in front of him. I leaned against the kitchen doorway. He looked up at me, and I could see by the look on his face that he knew he was eating one of my favourite breakfasts. Banana pancakes was my favourite, for sure, but I also loved toasted peanut-butter-and-molasses sandwiches. They would definitely be a close second.

I could eat all day.

I stood in silence watching Frankie stuffing banana pancakes. My mother's voice cut through that silent air and made my knees shake. "Ben, did you hear what I said! Go run the water!"

I think my mother enjoyed making me take a bath because she knew how much I hated it. I complained to her each and every time. But I had a secret I never told her. I kept it to myself. I didn't even tell Frankie, and I really wanted to tell someone. But because my mother loved making me suffer, I never told her that once I got into the tub of hot water, I liked it. It made my body warm, especially in the winter. I would make her call me ten times or more to get out of the tub and get dressed. But this wasn't winter, it was spring and it was the day Frankie was going to take me on a trip to see my dad at the electric company where he worked.

I came into my bedroom with a big bath towel around me. My mother was pulling clothes out of my dresser. She tossed onto my bed a tee-shirt, socks, underwear, a pair of jeans and my raincoat. Her voice snapped the whole time she tossed.

"Here, put some clean clothes on."

"Aw, Mum!"

"I want you to look your best when you see your dad."

My mum held my face in her warm hands, her eyes big as saucers. It was a look I had seen many times before. It was the 'kiss' look. She was going to kiss me. It wasn't anything new, because she was always kissing me. Sometimes she'd kiss me ten times in a row. Sometimes she would cover my face with kisses. Like she'd gone crazy or something. This looked like one of those crazy moments.

Frankie stuck his head in the door. "You ready to go, kid?"

"Don't you leave him alone out there," my mother said, never taking her eyes off me or letting go of my face.

"Ben, whadda ya think?" He stuck out a leg, showing off his shoes. "Got 'em at Banners!"

"Why do you always get brown shoes?" I looked over.

"Everybody wears black, kid, but brown, you gotta have confidence to wear brown." He snapped his fingers above his head like a dancer.

My mother's hands shook my head.

"Hey!" Then she pulled me to her and gave me one big kiss on my face and squeezed my face hard.

"Come on, let's go!" Frankie jumped into the room.

"I know you, Frankie. The Uptown Market is nearby. So, just don't." She tied the knot in my sneakers tighter than usual and looked up. "You mind your brother."

"I'll take care of him, Ma," Frankie whined.

I pulled my crisp, white tee-shirt over my head.

"Okay, let's go."

Frankie was going out the kitchen door ahead of me, into the back yard. From there we could go out the gate, down the laneway to Canning Street and the bus stop. It was exactly the way my father went to work every morning.

I felt my mother's hand on my arm as I was about to step out into the sunlight.

"Stop! Here, Frankie, take this to your dad." She handed him a brown paper bag neatly folded at the top.

"What's in the bag?"

"You wanna carry it?" Frankie looked at me.

"Sure."

Frankie handed me the bag.

"It's your father's lunch and a piece of chocolate cake." She tapped the top of my head.

"I better carry that," Frankie said, grabbing the bag out of my hand. "How many pieces in here, Mum?" She snatched the bag from his hand and cuffed him on the back of the head.

"Don't you dare!"

"What was that for?" he said, putting his hand on his head.

"If you'd been here last night you would have had some. Where were you?"

Frankie shrugged his shoulders.

"Ah, just out."

"Well, I don't like this 'just out'!" She cuffed him again.

Frankie stepped out into the yard with his hands planted in his pockets.

"You could give him brain damage." I looked up at my mother in the doorway. She looked determined.

"If he had one!" She stared out at Frankie in the yard. "But every time I cuff him all I hear is an echo!"

Frankie moved closer to the steps leading to the kitchen door.

"Okay, okay. I'll let you know next time. If it means that much to you."

"It does." She softened.

We all stood there for a few moments while Frankie and my mother looked at each other. I finally took the brown paper bag from my mother's hand and started across the back yard to the gate.

"Come on, Frankie, we're gonna miss the bus."

"Yeah … yeah."

"Ben, you make sure your father gets that cake," she yelled as the gate closed behind us.

The 32 bus stopped in front of a large, red-brick warehouse. As Frankie and I stepped off onto the sidewalk, we were faced with a tall green and white sign with the number 1003 on it and the words 'Main Entrance'. There was a guardhouse attached to the building with a man in a uniform sitting inside.

"That bag gettin' heavy?" Frankie's hand reached for the top of the brown paper bag in my hand. "Want me to carry it?"

"No. You'll eat it." I pulled the bag away.

"Ben, you gotta trust me. I'm your brother. When I say you can trust me, you can, you can trust me." He followed me. "Now, why would you say I'd eat it?"

"Cuz you eat everything."

The guard slowly got off his chair and stood over us, his hands on his hips, looming large in the doorway of the tiny house. He was dressed in a spotless uniform with the letters GE printed on his shirt.

"What do you two want?" He placed his hat on his head.

"I'm here to see my dad."

"And who would your dad be?" His voice was low and scary.

"Mr. Joe Flicker," Frankie shot back, his hands on his hips.

"Flicker." he reached for his clipboard. "Flicker.... Oh, Joe. Right. You go in that green door over there and he's way down at the end."

We walked away. I looked over my shoulder at the guard, who was going back into his tiny house.

"Frankie? Why do they have a guard?"

"I don't know. Top secret, I guess. Why do you ask?"

"They ain't got a gate!"

"Haven't got, 'ain't' ain't right."

"Why do you complain all the time?"

"I don't complain."

"Sure you do."

"Well, Ben, it's important to complain."

"Why's that?"

"How else you gonna let people know you don't like somethin'?"

The green door down at the end of the walkway had the words 'Warehouse Entrance B' written on it.

"Why won't you let me carry the bag?"

"Cuz it ain't heavy," I said with a smile.

"'Ain't' ain't right," he said shaking his head.

The big green door had one of those iron handles that you push down on. My thumb wasn't strong enough, so Frankie opened it. As we stepped inside, the large door slammed shut behind us. It was dark, much darker than my bedroom at night with the door closed. I raised my hand in front of my face and couldn't see my wiggling fingers. I couldn't even see the bag that I was holding onto. It was so quiet, all I could hear was my own breathing. It took a while for my eyes to adjust from the sunlight outside. Frankie put his hand on my shoulder. I jumped.

"What the…!"

"It's me, for God's sake!" He didn't sound too sure of himself.

The darkness made us both a little uneasy. I squinted and looked to the far end of the building and an office in the distance.

"Is that it?"

"Looks like it. Let's go."

We started to walk through the long passageway toward the office at the end of the hall. We passed row upon row of high shelves stacked with small cardboard boxes with the letters GE printed on the side. The concrete floor made the metal clips on the heels of Frankie's new shoes echo in the vast open space. Click/click, click/click. It was the only sound that could to be heard.

"Your shoes are loud."

"I gotta break them in first."

"Oh boy, you got taken."

"The sound of these shoes gives me confidence," he said, looking down the rows of boxes.

"Yeah? Well, you're never gonna sneak up on anyone in those. They'll hear you coming a mile away."

"They're not for sneakin' up, they're a girl thing…. Never mind, you're too young. You wouldn't understand." He did look real

confident as he spoke. "This is it." He put his hand on my chest.

The wooden door was painted grey with a large piece of frosted glass in the top half. Written in letters below the glass beside the door handle was, 'Lighting Department'. A closed venetian blind hung on the inside of the frosted glass. I reached for the handle.

"Hey, what are you doing?" Frankie slapped my hand away. "We have to knock."

"But Dad's in there!"

"Still have to knock." He cocked his head. "You do it."

I knocked.

"Yes! Come in." My father's voice was muffled through the door.

Frankie reached for the handle and the door swung open. The room was big. My dad was sitting behind a big brown wood desk at the far end of the room. It was surrounded floor to ceiling with shelves separated into little compartments. A tall wooden ladder with rollers on the top hung from a track that circled the room.

Hanging low over the centre of his desk was a green metal dome shade with a single light bulb.

"Boys!" He came rushing toward us. His arms wrapped around us in a big hug.

"Hi, Dad, we brought you some cake." I held the brown paper bag out in front of me.

"Cake, huh?"

"Chocolate. Frankie tried to eat it on the way here but I saved it for you." I could feel the side of Frankie's new shoe against my leg.

"Thank you, son. You know how much I love your mother's cake." He smiled and took the bag. "Come on in, sit down."

I moved quickly and sat in the large leather chair opposite his desk. Frankie moved slowly, his shoes clicking against the concrete floor. He sat on the corner of the desk.

"What's that sound?"

"Frankie's new shoes," I replied.

"New shoes!" He looked over at Frankie.

"How's work, Pop?" Frankie brushed something off the front of his pant leg.

"Oh, same old thing."

I looked around the room at the shelves. "What's in all those boxes, Pop?"

The phone on the desk rang. He picked it up and put the phone to his ear.

"Yeah. Okay. Where? Building C. Got it." He placed the handle back in the cradle. He got up, went over to the ladder and rolled it all the way around to the opposite side of the room. He started to climb but each step seemed painful. He stopped for a moment.

"Want some help, Pop?" Frankie moved toward the ladder.

"Naw, I do this all day long. No problem." The ladder started to shake as he got half way up. Frankie moved quickly to steady it.

"You okay?"

"Fine … fine."

He climbed up a few more steps to the top. I watched him with a touch of fear. He didn't have Frankie's confidence. He grabbed one of the small cardboard boxes from the shelf and began to come down, his foot searching for the step below.

"Toss that box down. I'll catch it."

Frankie's free hand reached out. My dad let go of the box. Frankie caught it, keeping a tight grip on the ladder with his other hand.

"Thanks, son."

"You should get them to fix that thing."

"Oh, just part of the job."

Frankie moved around the desk and winked at me.

"Hey, Pop. Is it okay if I go over to the market for a half hour or so?"

"You go ahead, I'll take Ben on my rounds." He picked up a canvas bag, put it over his shoulder and placed the box inside.

"You sure?"

"Yeah, go ahead."

"I'll be back." He quickly moved to the door. Then he began to run. I could tell by the sound of his new shoes.

"Come on, Ben."

Dad and I walked out of the office and through the large, dimly-lit warehouse.

"Mum told him not to go to the market."

"Well, let's not tell her, okay?"

"Okay. What's in those boxes, Dad?" I pointed down the rows of shelves.

"Light bulbs."

"What do you do with them?"

"Well, it's my job to make sure that if a bulb in the ceiling burns out anywhere in this warehouse, it gets changed with one of these from the boxes." He quickly pointed to the box in the canvas bag. Then, using his shoulder, he flipped the bag onto his back.

"Oh." I think my father sensed my disappointment.

"It's very important cuz if the lights don't work people can't see what they're doing. Could be very dangerous."

"You're in charge?"

"I'm in charge." I felt a confidence in my father's voice, the same confidence that Frankie has when he clicks his heels.

"Where are we going?"

"Building C." My father's pace quickened. I could hardly hear us walking through the warehouse. Our shoes touched the concrete but they made no sound.

"How come it's so quiet?" I reached out and took my father's hand.

"Not like Frankie's shoes, eh?" He smiled and shook his head. "Oh, that boy!" The air came out of him slowly like a whistle, getting quiet and then becoming no sound at all. "It's Saturday." He drew a deep breath. "Nobody works on Saturday."

"'Cept you."

"Ah huh."

His hand wiped his cheek.

This was the first time I noticed the marks on his hands. His hands were long and thin with dark veins showing. His skin looked like a glove that was two sizes too big. The knuckles were very red on the tops.

"Dad, why is your hand like that?"

"Like what?" He gazed at his hand. "Beat up? Just life, son."

He stopped and looked down one of the rows. He pointed up to the ceiling. "There. You see it, Ben?"

"Sure do, Pop, 'bout halfway down."

We walked quietly down toward the burned-out light. We said nothing, but I felt for the first time in my life that I was walking with my father. Just the two of us, saying nothing because there was nothing to say. It was just me and my dad, holding hands.

There was a tall A-frame wooden ladder leaning against one of the shelves. I looked up to the burned-out light. And it seemed pretty far away.

"Well, here we are."

My eyes were still on the dark light bulb in the ceiling. "You going up there, Pop?"

"Have to. I'm in charge."

I said nothing, because there was nothing left to be said. My father pushed the canvas bag to his back and began to climb. His steps were unsteady and the ladder began to shake. I was scared to do anything. I looked up at him. He waved for me to come closer.

"Ben? Do you think you could hold the ladder for me?"

"You bet, Dad," I felt my body move faster than it had ever moved. I seized the ladder with both hands.

"Keep her steady."

He began to climb again. When he reached the top he took the old bulb out of the socket and stuffed it in his bag. He got out the new one, put it in the socket and the light came on.

"Way to go, Pop!" I was relieved, not because he had changed the light bulb, but because he was still up there.

Then I heard the words I dreaded. "Comin' down."

I grabbed the ladder with even more purpose as my father climbed down, slowly, one step at a time. When we faced each other at the bottom of the ladder, he put his hand on my shoulder and tapped it three times.

"Let's go back."

We walked back to his office, my father's arm wrapped around me, his hand resting on my shoulder.

"How 'bout we eat that chocolate cake?"

"Sure." I couldn't answer fast enough.

"Well, we better get to it before Frankie gets back."

He opened the brown paper bag, reached inside and pulled out a sandwich made of dark rye bread with large slices of ham and cheese hanging over the edges. It was neatly wrapped in wax paper. He held the bag open, reached in and out came a metal container. He placed it on the desk, took the top off and inside was a large piece of chocolate cake sitting on one of our kitchen plates. He placed the cake on the desk under the light, reached into a drawer and brought out a knife. He turned the volume up on the radio. There was a baseball game on. As he was about to cut the cake in half, he reached out and offered me the knife.

"Here, you cut it. These aren't working too good today," he slapped his hands together.

"You like hockey, don't ya, Pop?" The blade sliced through the tender cake.

"Yup, but I love baseball." He unwrapped his sandwich and spread the wax paper out on his desk.

"Frankie says it's too slow."

"But Frankie has loud shoes," he laughed. "Baseball is a thinking-man's game."

"What do they think about?"

"Everything." His voice became excited. He took one piece of the cake and placed it on the wax paper in front of him. "What pitch to throw? How fast would the runner on first be? Is the batter a home-run hitter? Who's the guy on deck? What's the pitcher's strike-out pitch? And what pitch to throw for a ground ball double-play? That kind of thinking."

I had no idea my father knew so much about one thing. It was the longest speech I ever heard him say.

"Did I miss anything?" Frankie appeared at the door.

"Lunch."

"But not dessert." He looked down at my piece of cake. I quickly put my arms around it.

"Here, you can have some of mine." My father pushed the wax paper toward him.

"That's okay, Pop," Frankie gently pushed back the wax paper. "I had something at the market. Come on, Ben, we gotta get back."

I got up went around the desk and wrapped my arms around my dad's neck.

My dad looked up at Frankie. "What, no hug for your old man? You, with the noisy shoes."

Frankie didn't hesitate. He came round the desk and we both buried my father's face in our arms. I heard Frankie mumble in my father's ear, "Love ya, Pop."

Frankie and I retraced our steps back to the bus stop.

"What's with Dad's hands?" I sat down on the bench.

"I don't know. Ask Mum." He sat down next to me.

"Don't you know?"

"What's wrong with 'em?"

"They're beat up."

"He's old! I think he's fifty."

I let that sink in.

"That's old." We sat on the bench in silence. Nothing was said because there was nothing left to be said.

As we got to the front door of our house, Frankie caught my arm.

"Can you keep the market thing to yourself?"

"Don't tell Mum?"

"She'll just get mad for nothing. You know her." I could see he was desperate.

"I wanna play baseball this summer. Will ya take me?"

"Baseball!" His voice broke. "It's too slow. I thought you loved hockey!"

"It's a thinking-man's game."

"You've been talking to Pop."

"I won't tell Mum if you take me to baseball."

"You're already thinkin' too much."

"All summer," I warned.

The smells from the kitchen filled the house. My mother was making bread on the table. Her knuckles pushed down into the dough, crushing it onto the table over and over again.

"What's wrong with Dad's hands?"

"What's wrong with them?" She stopped suddenly.

"They're beat up."

"It's just life, dear." She went back to kneading the dough.

"That's what he said."

"He did?"

"Do everyone's hands end up like that?"

"That's nothing for you to worry about." She formed the dough into a big ball, placed it in the bottom of the bowl and covered it with a damp dishtowel.

"I'm going to play baseball this summer," I broke the silence.

"How come?"

"Frankie said he'd take me."

"Wait, let me catch my breath.... Frankie volunteered?

"Yup. We got a deal."

"You know your father loves baseball." She went over to the jam cupboard and picked up an old wedding photo, a photo I'd seen many times. It was taken in front of the brick doorway of their first house.

My mother was dressed in her long coat, her hands in her pockets. She was looking straight ahead with not much expression on her face. My father was in a double-breasted pinstripe overcoat with a white shirt, tie and hat. His hands hung by his side.

The Boy with the Dirty Face

IT WAS THREE DAYS BEFORE CHRISTMAS, and the snow was falling in thick, heavy flakes. On this, the last day before the holidays, the clock on the wall above the large blackboard in my second-grade classroom was ticking down to three o'clock.

"No running! Eugene, let go of Millie's hair! Stop running!"

Sister Mary Francis's voice could hardly be heard over the sound of everyone rushing to the door.

"If you don't stop pushing and running, I'll keep you all here until three-thirty! Eugene!"

I was one of the last to leave because I broke my bootlace. Sister Mary Francis re-laced my boot and I ran out of the classroom as fast as I could.

"Benjamin Flicker!" I looked back.

"Oh, never mind!" She collapsed into the seat of my desk. "Go!"

When I arrived home, my mother was in the kitchen. I loved the kitchen in winter because it was warm. The big iron wood-burning stove in the centre made sure of that. A large pot of stew was steaming on the stove as my mum added the remaining pieces of beef, chopped up cabbage and carrots. I didn't care much for cabbage. To me it smelt like Frankie's hockey socks.

There was the scent of maple walnut fudge in the air. Frankie was sitting at the kitchen table with a big wooden spoon, scraping up what was left of the fudge from the sides of the bowl.

"Here, Frankie, take this over to the church." My mother handed him a bag of pancake mix.

"Do I have to do it now?"

"Yes. Now!"

"Why doesn't Ben go? Hey, Ben! You wanna take this over?"

"Who's it for?"

"Ben already took food," she barked at him.

"Yes, that's right. I did!"

A week earlier I was asked to bring food to my school for the poor. I was in grade two and knew nothing about poor people but I thought it was a good idea because of George over on the next block. I thought George must be poor because George's face was always dirty.

"George, you got a dirty face," I would say whenever I saw him. In case he didn't know, he'd want to clean it off. Sometimes I would just move my lips and point to my face, "George, you got a dirty face."

"Will the poor people be there when you go?"

"That's not how it works," Frankie licked the spoon. "You don't get to give it to the poor yourself."

"Oh?"

"No. See, once the school collects your food they take it to the church. Father McNeil sort's it and he delivers it. He takes the all credit."

"Frankie!" My mother's voice had a warning tone. Frankie dropped the spoon and skipped out of the kitchen.

I remembered my choice of charity was a big can of Clark Beans cooked in maple syrup because they were my favourite. It was important to me that the poor person that got my can of beans would know who the giver was, in case they wanted to thank me.

So I got out a pen and wrote on the can, '4-U-Ben'.

When I got up the next morning, two days before Christmas Eve, the snow was falling in flakes as big as my hand. After breakfast Frankie took me to the ice rink at the corner of my street.

When we arrived all my friends were there in their hockey gear. There was Joseph, who lived down the street and was the richest kid I knew because one Christmas he got a set of cowboy guns that shot caps in a roll. And, of course, Eugene, who lived next door. And George. Dirty-face George. He played with his bare hands because he had no gloves.

We played for hours. Frankie watched from the side of the boards, talking to one of his girlfriends. I didn't score any goals and I played really hard. I heard Frankie calling me, "Hey, Ben! We gotta go! I'm freezin'!"

"I didn't score a single goal, Frankie."

"Well, there's always tomorrow. Come on, let's go."

I could hardly stand I was so tired. Frankie lifted me up and carried me, and on the way home, I rocked to sleep on my brother's shoulders. It was evening when I woke up in my favourite armchair in front of the iron stove in the kitchen. I was dressed in Frankie's old cowboy pajamas and my mum was making Christmas meat pies. I wanted to help but I was still too tired.

I heard someone banging on the front door. People always banged on the front door because there wasn't any doorbell. I ran to the door, opened it and Father McNeil was standing there holding a big cardboard box.

"It's the turkey!" I yelled. "Mum, hurry up! It's the turkey!"

"Merry Christmas, Mrs. Flicker!"

"And a Merry Christmas to you, Father."

I followed my mum back down the hallway. She stopped.

"What's the matter with you, you born in a barn? Close the door, you're letting all the heat out!"

I wasn't born in a barn so I went back and closed the front door.

In the kitchen we emptied the box onto the table. I loved digging into that box every Christmas. It had potatoes, carrots, onions, a box of saltines, Christmas candles and a loaf of white bread all on top of a large turkey. And under the turkey in the corner of the box was a big can of beans in maple sugar. I rushed to get the opener, and as I turned the can, some faint letters began to appear.

'4-U-Ben!'

Why did I get my beans back? I immediately thought I should get 'em to the poor people.

Then my heart stopped!

I must be one of those poor people I took food to school for. I was confused.

"Mum, are we poor?" She was chopping cabbage.

"We don't have much money, if that's what you mean."

"Oh...." I stuck my hands in my pockets and stared at the floor. I began to evaporate in the thin air.

I was poor!

"How can I go back to school? They all know I got a turkey in a box!"

My mum stopped what she was doing and came toward me at the end of the table.

"Does it really bother you, Ben?"

"I'm devastated!"

"You're what? Oh, you're devastated!"

My mum sat across from me and smiled. It wasn't often I saw my mum smile. She softly touched my forehead with her fingertips which were covered with white flour.

"Ben, look at me."

I looked up and stared into the sky-blue pool of my mother's eyes.

"Did you think you were poor before?"

"No."

"Then why do you think it's any different now? You're still the same Ben, aren't you?"

"No! Cuz now I'm just like George on the next block, 'cept I don't have a dirty face."

She sat up straight in her chair and her smile was gone.

"Well, you remember this, Ben: just because you have no money doesn't mean you're worth less than anyone else. Same as if you had a lot of money: that doesn't mean you're worth more than anyone else. It's what you make of your life, Ben, that's what has worth." She gently wiped the baking flour off my forehead. "So, if it bothers you that much, Ben, you've got your whole life ahead of you to do something about it."

Then she picked up the can of beans.

"Maybe this was opportune. Do you know what that means?"

"No."

"Well, it could mean, you getting this can of beans is a sign, and that gives you the opportunity to change things for yourself."

"So, I'm poor?"

"Well, poor is the wrong word."

"Well, what am I then?"

My mum let out a big sigh.

"You're not deprived or unfortunate or underprivileged. You're just broke. And when you grow up, you'll have the opportunity to do something about that. Okay? Now, why don't you help me finish the pies and put them in the oven?"

She put her finger on my lips to try and stop my next question.

"Can I keep the beans?"

"Of course you can."

She wrapped one of her aprons around me, tying the strings in a big bow.

"Fill 'em up."

I gripped the big spoon and began to scoop up the meat from the frying pan and fill the pie shells.

I said, after some thought, “Maybe next time I see George, I won’t mention his dirty face.”

Old Lady Beer

IN MY FATHER'S EYES, my star fell at 1:23 p.m. on the 26th of June. It was the day the shed burnt down. I was five years old and Eugene, who was known as Blueberry, was my best friend. He loved blueberries with a passion. He loved them so much that it prompted my mother to remark that it was a miracle his skin hadn't turned blue considering the quantity of blueberries that he consumed.

During that time, everyone in the neighbourhood had to find hiding places for their blueberries because of Eugene. In the early days of blueberry season, Blueberry could smell a blueberry pie cooking from a block away and when he found it cooling on an open window sill, it would be devoured within minutes and only the crumbs would be left to signal his visit. When the word was sent that Blueberry was out, the sound of windows closing could be heard throughout the neighbourhood.

On this day early in the blueberry season, Blueberry and I were asked to perform an errand we'd done many times before.

Mrs. Curran lived on the other side of the lane on the second floor. In summer, she would sit in her window looking out, watching people on the lane. She never combed her hair or changed her clothes. Blueberry told me once he heard that she never slept either. This day she gave us some money and asked us to go to the grocery store to pick up a quart of Dow. It was her favourite beer. The reason we never called her Mrs. Curran was because she drank a Dow a day. So, we called her Old Lady Beer.

She hated going to the grocery on the corner, so Blueberry and I became her closest friends. We ran across the street, picked up a quart of Dow in a brown paper bag and returned as fast as we could. Speed was of the essence with Old Lady Beer. The faster we performed the task, the larger the reward got. But on this particular day when we returned, Old Lady Beer was nowhere to be found

Blueberry and I stood in her kitchen and stared down at the change on the table. $4.35. Now $4.35 was a lot of money to us and it could buy of a lot of black licorice. I don't know what came over us, but we took the money and returned to the grocery. Once we got there we realized that there was a lot more we could buy with $4.35 besides black licorice. For instance, there was a blueberry birthday cake with blueberry icing.

As we sat in my father's carpentry shed in the back yard, Blueberry and I lit the candles as we giggled with glee at our prize. Blueberry looked over at me and began to sing. "Happy Birthday you and me, Happy Birthday you and me, Happy Birthday to us!" we yelled out, laughed and blew out the candles. Blueberry blew so hard that he blew one of the candles clean off the top of the cake to the other side of the shed and that made us laugh even harder as we grabbed chunks of cake and stuffed them into our mouths.

"Do you have any money left?" Blueberry asked.

"Yes," I said. "Why?"

"I'm thirsty," he responded.

"You want me to get you some water?"

"No. I want a Pepsi," he said.

So off we went back to the store to get our drinks.

As we joked our way back down the laneway on our way back

from the store, we noticed there was some black smoke in the air. When we turned the corner into the yard, my heart stopped. There was my father and my brother Will, slinging buckets of water from hand to hand putting out a fire where the shed once stood. The walls were gone. The only thing left standing was my father's charred workbench with the remains of a blueberry birthday cake sitting in the middle. The guilt was written all over us as our sticky fingers gripped our Pepsi bottles and our blueberry-stained mouths held a look of horror. Two little angels fell quickly in my father's eye.

"It's lucky for you that the shed wasn't up against the house, or the whole place would have burned to the ground!" my father shouted, as he tossed the remaining water in his bucket on the charred workbench.

He left it to Will to dish out the punishment; the charred tools were to become his some day.

"Do what you want with them," Dad said as he tossed the bucket to the ground and walked back into the house. Will pointed that scary finger and beckoned us to come closer. We stumbled our way across the yard in fear of what was to come, and as we stopped in front of Will, he leaned down and grabbed both Pepsis from our hands. He placed both bottles to his lips, threw his head back and downed each one until there wasn't a drop left. He burped the loudest burp I'd ever heard, then pointed that scary finger once again beckoning us to come even closer as he leaned down.

There we were, all three in a circle, nose to nose to nose, staring into each other's eyes. His eyes looked at my eyes and my eyes looked at his eyes. Then my eyes looked at Blueberry's eyes and Blueberry's eyes were looking at my eyes. Then Blueberry's eyes looked quickly at Will's eyes and Will's eyes were looking at his. Then I looked back at Will and Will looked back at me and Blueberry looked back at him and this went on for what seemed like an hour until I didn't know who to look at next. Finally, Will spoke.

"Well, boys! What am I going to do with you?" he asked in a quiet, calm tone.

"You could let us go," Blueberry said, without missing a beat.

"Let you go?" Will replied. "No, I don't think so." He then turned and looked into my eyes and said, "You know how much those tools meant to me. How could you do this, Skins?" I couldn't stop my lips from moving as I tried to explain. I told him that we took the money from Old Lady Beer, that we didn't mean to but we just wanted some of that black licorice over at the grocery and then that once we got there we changed our minds and bought a blueberry birthday cake instead, with candles. I removed the change from my pocket and showed him what was left.

"He made me do it!" I blurted out as my eyes darted toward Blueberry.

"No I didn't. I don't even like cake!"

Will thought a bit, looked both of us in the eye, took the money from my hand and said, "Okay, you two come with me." He took us over to the charred workbench. "Sit! And don't move until I get back!"

We quickly sat down opposite each other and watched Will as he disappeared down the brick laneway to Dominion Street. Blueberry and I didn't move a muscle as we sat and waited out of fear of what Will would do if he returned and we weren't there. Finally, Blueberry spoke.

"I didn't make ya do it," he said.

"Sure ya did," I said. "I wanted licorice. You wanted cake."

"Yeah, but you wanted candles." He looked at me and he seemed pleased with himself. Then, after a moment's pause, he said, "I seen Willy fight. He's gonna beat the be-Jesus out of you."

It seemed like forever as my thoughts turned to my brother Will ripping my arms out of my sockets and twisting my head off my shoulders until I was just a pile of body parts resting on the charred workbench. Old Lady Beer appeared on her back porch sipping that bottle of Dow, dressed in her well-worn pink terrycloth bathrobe that was tied tightly around her abundant middle. She looked down at these two little heads that were staring back at her.

"Whadda ya two boys sittin' in the middle-a-all that burnt wood for?"

"Do you want us to go to the store for you again? I could go for you right now, if you want," Blueberry quickly offered.

"Didn't ya just go?" Old Lady Beer slurred back, holding up the bottle of Dow.

"They certainly did!" Will shouted back as he entered the backyard carrying a large box in his arms and two bottles of Pepsi. Blueberry and I looked at each other as he approached. I hoped

my best friend couldn't see the terror in my eyes. Will placed the large box between us along with a bottle of Pepsi in front of our chins. I could hardly see Blueberry behind his bottle of Pepsi as my brother's hands reached in and flipped open the top of the box to reveal the biggest birthday cake I'd ever seen. Slowly he lit the candles.

"Well, since you guys didn't get to celebrate, I thought I'd pick you up a couple of cigars to top off your meal." At which point he produced two huge, long cigars and stuck one in each of our mouths.

"Is someone's birfday?" Old Lady Beer slobbered from her perch.

"Oh yes! A very big celebration!"

"Why did ya burn down the shed?" She leaned down and placed her elbows on the gallery railing.

"Thank you, Mrs. Curran," he smiled and waved back at her.

"Happy birfday!" She waved back. She stood up and disappeared into her house.

Will then cut into the cake and placed a piece on the charred table in front of us.

"Okay boys, eat up!"

"Could I have a fork?" Blueberry whined as Will opened each bottle and produced a match for our cigars. Before he would let us go, he made us finish the cake, the Pepsis and the cigars. We must have looked like mad fools eating cake with our hands, gulping down our Pepsis and puffing on those big, stinky cigars. As the colour in our cheeks turned to green, Will smiled down at us.

"How's the cake, boys?"

The Black Tie

My mum is always busy, but when Christmas comes along it's like she has ten hands, and that Christmas wasn't any different. All she was doing was baking in the kitchen, ironing my play clothes, washing the dishes and yelling at Frankie to put out the garbage. She never yelled at me.

When I got up it was still dark. It was Christmas morning. I rushed from the bedroom that I shared with Frankie and screeched to a halt in the middle of the kitchen floor. There was a decorated Christmas tree in the far corner. I didn't know how it got there because it wasn't there the night before. Our stuffed Christmas stockings hung on a mantle Will had made a few days earlier. And there was one for each of us. It was my first Christmas stocking, so that sock kept drawing me closer and closer. I stuck my hand inside and began to pull out the contents onto the floor: One large onion, four long carrots, three fair-sized potatoes and a small head of cabbage, which was not my favourite vegetable.

Finally, as I dug as deep as I could into the toe of the sock, I gripped the prize between my fingers and hauled it up. My treasure was in the shape of a nickel but bigger. My heart began to pound just thinking of Lavois' grocery store on the corner with its five-for-a-penny candy. I looked closer at the coin in my hand.

It wasn't a nickel at all. It had a moose on the back. Nickels have a beaver. I was excited.

But what were all the vegetables for? Was I the only one who got them? I investigated the other socks and they were all filled with vegetables just like mine. Will's sock had a big turnip, which I don't like, and Frankie's had a head of cauliflower, which I don't like. Maggie's sock was full of carrots, which I do like, a lot. Of all the vegetables my mum makes me eat, I could eat carrots all day long. Winn's sock looked empty; she didn't like vegetables at all.

I dug deeper to see if there were any more mooses but I was the only one who got one. I began to tremble at the thought that maybe I was supposed to eat all those vegetables before I could spend the booty from the bottom of my sock. My fears were put to rest when my mother entered and stared at me with a little smile that wasn't quite a smile, but I guess it was the best she could do at 5 a.m.

"You just couldn't wait, huh?" She moved to the stove and put the kettle on.

"Hey ma, what are all these vegetables for?" She looked at me a moment. It wasn't a long moment. It didn't have to be for me to get the idea that my question was unwanted.

"Pick those vegetables up off the floor, wash them, then put them in that pot."

I began to do as I was told for fear she'd find out about the moose.

"Are we going to eat them?"

My mother turned and smiled, "Benjamin, we eat everything."

"Joseph Vanier doesn't have to eat 'em."

"How do you know that?"

"Cuz he's rich."

It's true. Joseph was the richest kid I knew.

He lived a couple of blocks over from me on St. Antoine Street.

That street was fancy. It had trees. You had to walk up a flight of outside stairs and then a flight of inside stairs to get into to his house. His house was made of big grey stone. My house was made of dirty red brick.

Joseph got a new set of Hopalong Cassidy cowboy cap-guns for Christmas the year before. They were black with silver cows on the holsters, and a thick wide black belt and silver buckle. The silver guns had Hoppy's picture on the black handles and the guns shot caps in a roll. Rapid fire. Every time you pulled the trigger, a spark shot out the back. When I told my mother about them and how great they were, she told me not to get my heart set on getting them for Christmas anytime soon. "Too much money," was the last thing she muttered.

I told her about Joseph's dad wearing a shirt and tie every day. She told me that Mr. Vanier worked in an office downtown. Whenever I was at Joseph's house near dinnertime and his dad would come home, it was always fun to see which tie he had on for that day. Sometimes his tie was red, sometimes blue, or sometimes green with designs on it. Not like my dad, who wore a dark blue shirt with the same colour dark blue pants every day. I only once saw Mr. Vanier wear a black tie and that was the day Joseph's grandfather died from a heart attack. Joseph cried the whole day, that day. He never once played with his cap-guns.

I remember that black tie because one morning a few months earlier my oldest brother, Robert, came into the kitchen. He put his arm around my mother and kissed her on the forehead. She was standing at the window looking out into the backyard, not saying a word. She was dressed in her black dress that she usually wore when she went out singing down at The Dominion. As Robert turned toward me, I noticed he was wearing a black tie. When my brother Will came into the kitchen he was also wearing a black tie. My sister Winn was wearing a black dress and I didn't know she even had one. Frankie was wearing Will's old dark blue suit, which now fit him perfectly and a dark navy-blue tie. My other sister, Maggie, who was eight years old, and was the one who looked after me when I needed looking after, was dressed in her black school uniform.

"For God's sake, Maggie." Will just shook his head.

"It's the only black I have."

"Let her be, Will." Winn touched Maggie's arm. "I'll give you my black sweater to cover up the white blouse."

They all sat quietly around the kitchen table, everyone looking over at my mum. There was no talking, no laughter. Tears were falling down my mother's cheeks. It was so quiet. Even her crying made no sound.

"What's for breakfast, Mum?" I asked, leaning on the table.

Robert looked over at me. "Come on, Ben, let's get you dressed."

"Are we not having breakfast?"

"We will, a little later. Come on." Robert took my hand and slowly walked me back to my bedroom.

"Where are your good clothes?"

"My Sunday clothes?"

"Yeah, Sunday clothes." He put his hand on the top of my head.

"Bottom drawer."

"Get 'em out. Let's put them on."

"It isn't Sunday, Robert."

"Yes, I know. But today we have to pretend it's Sunday. Okay?"

I went over to my small dresser in the corner of the room and pulled out the bottom drawer. My Sunday clothes, which took up the entire drawer, were there, very neatly folded by my mother. I had no dark clothes, so I put on Frankie's old grey long pants, dark socks, white shirt, blue sports jacket and brown shoes.

Robert looked down at me and smiled. "You're getting to be quite a young man."

"Frankie's stuff fits me perfectly," I said with a grin.

"Wait right here. Don't move. I'll be right back."

I waited. Robert came back into my room carrying a black tie.

"I think you should wear this." He put the tie around my neck.

"Can you make it just like yours?"

"Yes, I can." He slowly began to make the knot in my tie, then

stopped, undid it and sat on the edge of my bed and pulled me close to him.

"I told Mum that I wanted to be the one to tell you this." He wiped his face with his hands. He took out a hankie from his pocket and rubbed his palms. "Something … something has happened to Dad." He again used the hankie to wipe his forehead and his eyes. Then he went quiet.

"What, Robert?"

"You know Dad has not been home over the last few days. And … well … he died, a couple of days ago, very suddenly. A heart attack."

"That means I don't have a dad anymore, right?"

"Well, you've got me." He gently finished the knot in my tie and tucked it under my chin. "And you've got Will and Frankie."

"Not the same, is it Robert?"

He looked down at me. "No. … No, it's not."

"I don't feel good, Robert."

He looked down at the floor. "I need you to be strong, Ben. I need you to be really strong." He cupped my face in his hand. Tears were beginning to fall down his cheeks. "Can you do that?" He used his hankie and wiped a tear from my cheek.

"I will, Robert. I will."

He wiped his own eyes with his hankie and stood up. He put his arm around my shoulder. "Let's go join the family."

We walked out of the bedroom and down the hall toward the kitchen.

At the church, my dad was lying in a coffin in front of the altar with the top opened so you could see his face. Robert sat beside me on the bench along with Winn, Frankie, Maggie and Will. My mum was sitting in the pew in front of me, alone. There were lots of people in the church sitting around us.

"Who are all these people? Did they come for the Mass?"

Robert put his hand on my shoulder. "They're all friends of Dad's or people who knew and liked him. They've come to pay their respects."

"Did you pay respects?"

"Yes. I saw Dad in the hospital just before he died."

"Did Winn and Frankie and Maggie and Will?"

"Yes. They did."

"Can I could go up and see him in the box?"

"Is that what you'd like to do?"

"I'd like to pay respects, too."

Robert stared down at me. "Want me to go with you?"

I shook my head and Robert stepped back and I squeezed by him into the centre aisle. I looked at my mother as I passed her but her head was down and she didn't see me. I continued to walk slowly up the aisle glancing at the people sitting on either side. Some smiled. Some nodded.

My dad was always smiling. When I would get up on a cold morning, he was always there in the kitchen by the fire in the stove, his arms stretched out waiting for me to climb onto his knee and keep warm.

When I got up beside the box, I realized that it was high above my head. I couldn't see my father's face at all. So I reached up and gripped the side of the box, pulled myself up on my toes and looked inside. But all I could see was the tip of my father's nose.

Then I felt two hands on my waist lifting me up. I looked around and there was Robert holding me up high. I looked down into the box at my dad. He was lying there dressed in a dark blue suit, light pink shirt – his favourite colour – and a white tie. His face was pale white, almost as white as his tie. My dad's old brown wooden rosary rested between his fingers.

"Go ahead Ben. Pay your respects."

"I'm never going to see him again, am I Robert?"

"No." He looked at me, his blue eyes full of tears. "Never again."

I stared into my brother's watery eyes. "Be strong, Robert."

He smiled and gently nodded.

I looked back down at my dad lying there in his blue suit. I reached out my hand and touched his chest. "Bye, Pop."

Robert lowered me to the floor and we walked back to our seats holding hands. I looked around at the big church and all its coloured windows. I'd been here every Sunday with my mum for Mass. But this wasn't Sunday and the church was only half full. As I passed my mum, she looked up at me and reached out her hand. "Here, Ben. Come, sit with me."

Robert let go and I slid in beside her. She wrapped her arm around me and pulled me tight to her. I could feel her fingers pressing into my skin. She leaned down and kissed the top of my head. And before I knew it people started to stand and the box with my dad in it was rolling down the centre aisle. We sat there side by side, my mother hugging me tightly the whole time. As the box passed us, we stood and walked out of the church. It was over.

The Christmas music was playing on the radio and my mother looked down at me sitting on the floor. "Ben, after you finish putting the clean vegetables in the pot, can you wait on the gifts and help me with the toast for breakfast?"

"Yeah," I said dejectedly.

Maggie came into the kitchen rubbing her eyes. "Why is everyone up so early and making so much noise?"

"Sorry, Maggs. You go back to bed." Mum then whispered to me, "And you butter the toast."

"Who decorated it?" Maggie said, as she stumbled toward the Christmas tree.

"Robert did before he left last night," Mum answered quietly.

"He left for the rest of his life without saying good-bye!"

I stopped buttering. "Where did he go?"

"He got a job in Halifax."

"Just like him, so secretive." Maggie growled, looking at the tree.

My mother looked over at my sister, who had a sad look on her face. "He left something for you."

"Who, me?" Maggie's voice got excited.

"Yes, Maggs, you."

"Is it okay if I look?" I watched as she went through all the gifts under the tree until she came to a small red box wrapped with gold ribbon, and read the note. "To Maggie. Merry Christmas, Robert."

She quickly glanced back at my mother. "Can I open it?"

"If you open one he'll want to open his." My mum looked down at me with the butter knife in my hand.

"So, what's wrong with that!"

"Nothing." She laughed. "Go ahead."

The words were hardly out of my mother's mouth and my sister had the gold bow off the box. She gently undid the red wrapping. "Oh, I hope it is, I hope is it! It is! It's a bracelet! Oh Mum, it's a bracelet!"

"It's beautiful." My mum moved over to where Maggie was sitting on the floor.

"I love it!" It wasn't the first time I saw tears in Maggie's eyes. She cried a lot. "How did he know?"

"Well, that's Robert. So secretive."

"What are you crying for? Ain't ya happy?" I looked at my sister sitting on the floor with my mother's arm around her.

"It's a girl thing, Ben." My mother smiled.

All of a sudden Maggie jumped to her feet. "I'm going to show Winn," she said, rushing out of the room.

"Well, that should start a rush to the tree." My mother looked up at me and had a big grin on her face.

"Something wrong, Mum?"

"Robert left something here for you, too. Right there."

I looked to the large box she was pointing at. It was wrapped in colour-comic-strip newspaper with a large rope tied around it.

"You wanna open it?"

"Can I?"

"I think you should." Her hand reached out and I placed the butter knife in her palm. "I'll take the toast, too."

I sat on the floor and my mum put the box in front of me.

"It's bigger than my lap," I said, staring at the rope that was tightly tied around the box.

"Go ahead," she nodded.

I pulled at the ends of the rope and it undid like a snake. I took off the paper carefully and saved the comics to one side. I opened the box and I couldn't believe my eyes. There in the middle of the wrapping paper was a set of Roy Rogers cowboy cap-guns. I looked up at my mum and began to cry.

"I guess it isn't just a girl thing." She wiped a tear off my cheek.

"Oh, Mum."

I took them out of the box and she helped me put them around my hips. Silver glistened off the holsters and the belt buckle. She tied the leather straps to my legs. I gripped the white-handled six-shooters. I looked down into the bottom of the box and there was a small red box of caps.

"He said they were only single shot. Whatever that means."

"Oh, I don't care. They're Roy Rogers." I reached for the caps and started to put them in the back of the gun.

"I think it's a little early for you to be shooting off caps. Do me a favour: let's have breakfast first."

"Winn's up!" Maggie raced into the room showing off her new bracelet.

"Hey, Maggs! Look what I got from Robert."

"Just what you wanted. Guns!" She said it as if it didn't matter to her at all.

We all moved to the kitchen table and helped with the breakfast, Maggie holding her arm in front of her like the Queen and me with my cap-guns hanging by my sides.

Winn came bolting into the room. "What about me?"

"You should look." Maggie pointed toward the tree, her bracelet hanging from her wrist.

My mother nudged me on the shoulder. "You know, Ben, he knew how much you wanted those cowboy guns and he saved up all year to get them for you. Do you know what that is?"

I shook my head, staring down at the cap-guns on my hips.

She lifted my chin with her finger. "Brotherly love."

Skinned Heads

I WAS FINALLY BECOMING A MAN, just like my older brothers. I was six years old and on my way to attend my first day at Belmont Elementary School, grade one. I was real excited.

I rushed into the room and picked a desk right at the front and sat down at my own desk. Something I didn't have to share with anyone.

Her name was Miss Thomas and she was my teacher. She spoke softly and smiled a lot. I smiled back from my front seat, hanging on her every word. She went to the blackboard and wrote down the three things she expected from us: one, we were to be on time every morning; two, no fighting in the classroom; and three, everybody, and she underlined the word 'everybody' with big chalk marks, takes a bath every day. Those kids who don't do number three would be sent home.

She then explained that we all had to go down to the nurse's room for a little check-up.

My eagerness to please placed me near the front of the line waiting outside the nurse's room. When I finally entered, I noticed two people dressed in white. One was sitting in a chair close to the door and the other was standing on the other side of the room with her hands resting on the back of the chair in front of her.

The one closest to the door had a small table beside her. On the table was a tall bottle full of wooden sticks, a bigger bottle full of cotton balls, a large bowl full of water and a small towel. The other person dressed in white also had a table beside her and on it was a pair of scissors, a whiskbroom and a metal dustpan.

The one closest to the door beckoned me to come forward. She opened my mouth, stuck one of the wooden sticks on my tongue, withdrew it abruptly then quickly threw it into the pail beside her. She grabbed my head, and with her thumbs, stretched my eyes open real wide and looked into them very intently. She held my head firmly, turned it and stuck some cotton balls in each of my ears, made them wet, then dug them out with her finger. The cotton balls joined the wooden stick in the pail beside her. She grabbed my head again and began to pick through my hair the way monkeys do at the zoo.

She suddenly stopped, stuck her hands in the bowl of water, wiped them on the towel and pointed me toward the woman and her whisk broom with one softly-spoken word. "Lice."

The woman with the broom sat me down in the chair in front of her. Without a word spoken she covered me up to my neck with a white sheet, picked up her scissors and started to cut my hair. Quickly it began to fall to the floor around me. I was scared. All I could see was my hair floating in the air like feathers around me. Then I heard that clipper sound you hear at the barber's. She gripped my head firmly. I felt it start at the back of my neck and it didn't stop until I looked up and saw my hair fall off the front of my forehead. Some of it rested on my nose and my eyelids. I tried to shake my head and get it off, but she had a firm grip. It was just one long stroke after another until she was done. She let go of my head and I slowly looked around. My hair was everywhere. She sprinkled some white power on my head, swiftly removed the sheet, told me I was done and patted me on the back. I couldn't move. I was stunned as she gently helped me up and ushered me toward the door.

The door closed behind me and I faced my classmates. I stared at them and they stared at the top of my head. I could smell the white powder on my scalp. I very slowly lifted my hand and touched the top of my head. My hair was gone and I didn't even know what lice were.

I ran down the hallway, out the door, across the schoolyard and home to tell my mother. She wasn't there, but Will was. He was out back in the toolshed fixing a chair leg. I ran into the shed.

"Holy shit! You're bald!"

"What's lice?" I blurted out.

"Ah.... They grow in your hair. Boy, they skinned you!"

"Are there lots of them?"

"Like cockroaches, once you see one...."

I shivered.

"Hey, they don't eat through your head, you know," he said. How did he know I was thinking that?

"Are you sure?"

"I'm positive," he smiled, resting the broken chair on the workbench.

"I want you to look."

"Sure," he said, moving toward me. His hands fearlessly touched my scalp. "I think lice live in your hair and that's why they cut it all off. It doesn't mean you got lice. They just don't want you to get 'em," he said, gently rubbing my scalp.

"They don't do this every day, do they?"

"No," he laughed. "Look at it this way, it's one less thing to wash in the morning."

"Yeah, but my teacher told me I still have to take a bath every day no matter what."

"Yeah, going to school's tough," he said rubbing my head with his hands. He turned back to the workbench and the broken chair leg. "Hey kid," he smiled, pushing his hand through his full head of hair, "pass me the glue, will ya?"

The next morning I was standing in my choo-choo-train pajamas in the middle of the bathroom. The steam rising from the basin was beginning to cloud the whole mirror. Will stood bare-chested.

"Ben." He touched my bald head. "Close the door so the steam don't get out and you and I will share the art of the blade, the brush and the cup."

I rushed to close it. It was fun to hear him talk.

"Soon you'll get to be a man, like me…," he said, lifting me up onto the warm radiator.

I nodded yes.

"Good," he said. "It's important to start off on the right foot. Now, to be in the right frame of mind to shave, you got to have steam and you got to drop a smidgen of water into this cup."

I slowly poured the water into the cup.

"Just a smidgen, and work this fellow into a lather. Now, you don't have whiskers, do you?"

I shook my head.

"Well, I got whiskers. Big ones!"

He looked into the mirror, cupped his chin in his hands and with a fierce look in his eye said, "And they have got to go!" He looked back at me. "You wanna feel them?"

"Yes," I nodded.

"Okay," he said, and Will leaned all the way down to where I sat.

He was right. The biggest whiskers in the world were there. Right there in front of me. Face to face we stared at each other for the longest time.

"Well, go on, touch 'em!" he finally said. "But," he warned, "don't hurt yourself."

I reached out with both hands and cupped his face.

"Go on, feel 'em all!"

I ran my hands all over Will's face.

"Well, what do ya think?" he smiled.

I looked deep into his hazel eyes.

"They gotta go!" I yelled.

"Right," he said, and passed in front of me the brush and the Old Spice cup with the sailboat on the front. With that twinkle in his eye and determination in his voice, he said, "Take no prisoners!"

With that I reached into the cup with the brush and covered his face with the white lather, not just his whiskers, but also his whole face, every inch. And when I was through, he laughed his hearty laugh and grabbed me in his gruff, loving way.

"You kill me, kid. You really do."

He stood with the blade in his hand, wiped the steam off the mirror and began the tale of Elmer Jones.

As he told the story, he spoke faster and faster and so did the speed of his shaving.

Now Elmer Jones woke at dawn,
Put his huntin' britches on,
Looked up at the shotgun on the wall
He decided then and there
To bag himself a hunk of bear
And hang that old bear's hide upon the wall.
Now he ate his breakfast, slopped the hogs,
Kissed his wife, called the dogs,
Picked up his gun and started on his quest.
He crossed the crick and hit the trees,
Threw back his head and sniffed the breeze,
Let out a yell and pounded on his chest.
Now he hunted all the morning through,

But not a bear came into view,
And Elmer's thoughts were on the kitchen range,
'Cause he was sick as he could be
Of lamb and chicken fricassee
And he needed a mess of bear meat for a change.
Now Elmer's mind was in a fog,
And he paused and sat down on a log
To get his faculties back in a groove.
He heard a noise and standing there
Before him was a grizzly bear.
He decided it was time he made his move.
So Elmer's shoulders sprouted wings,
His feet developed inner springs.
To linger longer, he was disinclined.
He ran so fast through muck and mire,
His ankles set his socks on fire,
And still the bear kept comin' on behind.
Now a deer with antlers eight feet wide,
Got in the way of Elmer's stride,
Both of them were heading for the brush.
And Elmer said, "Now listen, son,
If that's as fast as you can run,
Just move it over, this boy's in a rush!"
Now the bear was gainin' inch by inch,
And soon he reached out for the clinch.
Elmer saw the fence around his place.
He ran so fast and jumped so hard
He went sixty feet across the yard
And slammed the kitchen door in the bear's face.
Now the bear was tryin' to get inside
And Elmer sought a place to hide.
And Mrs. Jones began to pull her hair.

She said, "This fuss has gotta stop.
Why don't you just let the matter drop?"
He said, "Honey, go and tell that to the bear!"
She said, "Now listen, you big goon,
How come you think you're Daniel Boone?
Is that the only bear meat you could find?"
He said, "I'm sure that you're aware
That Daniel always kills his bear.
Yeah, but honey, I done brought mine home alive!"

"Elmer and the Bear"— Phil Harris

When he finished the story, he finished shaving, wiped off the excess lather with a towel and looked into the mirror. "It's a crime they made me so handsome!"

We both laughed.

My sister Winn's high pitched "Hurry up!" came from the hall, accompanied with a fist on the bathroom door that got our attention. I was still smiling as Will opened the door. I watched as the steam was quickly sucked out into the hallway and the cool morning air.

The Spelling Bee

SPELLING IS AGONY. I spell words the way they sound, which most of the time is not the way they're spelled at all. Almost every day there would be a spelling test in my grade four class. When my name was called, my heart would start to pound and my legs would shake as I walked through the rows of desks to the front of the class. My teacher wore a long black habit with a silver cross hanging around her neck. There was a white trim around the hood on her head. I don't know if anyone else was afraid of her, but I was. Her name was Sister Anne.

One evening after supper I was in my room on the edge of the bed, sitting on my hands. I was ashamed to show my mother my hands because I knew she would be disappointed to know I couldn't spell. I was hoping that the pain of me sitting on them would take away the throbbing pain of Sister Anne's pointer.

"Are you sick or something?" My older brother Will's large frame filled the doorway.

"No."

"You didn't eat your dessert. That isn't like you."

"I'm okay." I sat harder on my hands.

"What's the matter, don't you like cake? Bought it specially for you."

He brought a plate out from behind his back and it had a piece of

chocolate cake on it.

I sat down harder on my hands, trying not to look at him.

"Are you mad at me for being away so long? I have to go north. It's the only way I can make money."

I shook my head and continued to look at the floor, my hands tucked tightly under me.

He took a step forward and stretched out the plate. "Here, have some. It's chocolate!"

I continued to look down at the floor, afraid to look up, afraid to get off my hands.

"I'm going north again in a couple of days. I'd hate to go thinking you're mad at me."

Finally, I looked up at him standing in the middle of the room, his arm stretched out holding the plate of chocolate cake.

"I love cake!" I shouted with tears in eyes.

"I know you do." He sat next to me on the bed.

"I love cake, Will! I really do! I love cake!" I looked up at him.

Will wiped a tear from my cheek with his thumb. "What is it, Ben? What's the problem, huh?" He put the plate on the floor and put his arm around my shoulder. He gently pulled me close to him, my face buried deep into his chest. "It's okay. It's okay. How 'bout some cake, huh?"

I looked up into his eyes and the sting of Sister Anne's pointer was far away as I lay safe in my brother's arms.

"I…. I can't hold my fork," I blurted out.

"What? What do you mean, you can't hold your fork?"

"My hands are sore." I was fighting back my tears.

"Show me."

I slowly backed away, gently pulled my hands out from under me, turned them over and showed him my scars. A blister in my palm had broken and the tips of my fingers were red and throbbing. I could hear my brother's breath get louder as anger swelled up in him. He reached over and held my hands open.

"Who did this to you?"

"Sister Anne."

"A nun?"

"Yes."

"Does Mum know about this?" Will placed his hand on the back of my head. "How often has this happened?"

"After every spelling test."

He turned away and sat there in silence for a few moments. His breath quickened.

"Is this the reason you've been skipping school?"

"Uh huh."

"How many days?"

"Five."

"I see. Ben, you're eight years old."

"Almost nine."

"Right. I know it's tough, but you've got to stay in school or you'll end up like me. No education gives you no chance for advancement except freezing your butt off in Frobisher Bay." He placed his hand on the top of my head and ruffled my hair. "Is that what you want? Huh? To end up like me?"

He didn't know how desperately I wanted to say yes, instead I shook my head no and he smiled.

"Is there someone I could talk to about this?"

"I don't think so. Gotta learn to spell."

"Promise me you'll go back tomorrow." I nodded my head.

"Good." He leaned down to the floor and picked up the plate. "What d'ya say we share this? I can't eat a whole piece myself and you'd be doing me a favour."

"Okay."

My brother picked up the fork and cut off a piece of the cake and turned the fork toward me. We sat there and shared the cake until it was finished, my brother feeding me. First me. Then him.

The next morning I walked to school as usual. When I arrived I was told to report to the principal's office. As I waited I got to thinking about those spelling tests. I began to sweat. The hair on my arm began to tingle so I got up and bolted out the front door to freedom.

After walking along St. Catherine Street for a couple of hours, I discovered the furniture department on the fifth floor of Eaton's department store. I picked out a nice, big, comfy chair facing the elevators and closed my eyes.

"Hey! Wake up!"

When I opened my eyes an older man with a nametag on his jacket that read 'Mr. Lacy' was staring at me.

"Aren't you supposed to be in school?"

"No. It's a holiday,"

"A holiday? What school do you go to?"

"Luke Callahan Memorial." I forgot to lie.

He pointed a finger and beckoned me. I got up and followed him into his office. Again, he used his finger to point at a chair opposite his desk.

"Sit." He picked up the phone. "What's your name?"

"Ben. Benjamin Flicker."

Mr. Lacy spoke quietly into the mouthpiece, then put the phone down and looked over at me. "They're on their way!"

We sat in silence. Mr. Lacy wagged his long finger at me.

"Ooooh!"

The time on the big Bulova clock on the wall read 2:10 p.m. when two large men appeared. They were both tall and fat with big, round bellies, wearing exactly the same suits – gray with a white shirt and black shoes. The only difference was their ties. One wore a plain, bright yellow tie and the other wore a tie with a dancing woman in a grass skirt on it.

"You looking for him?"

"You Benjamin Flicker?" Yellow Tie asked, pushing back his suit jacket. My eyes fixed on a gun on his hip. I nodded.

Mr. Lacy pointed at me, urging me, with his finger, to go with the man with the gun. So I did.

I sat in the front seat of the car between the two big men. They said nothing. Dancing Girl Tie concentrated on driving and Yellow Tie fiddled with the radio in the dash. He scowled down at me, his elbow almost touching to my cheek. The seat was so low I could hardly see out the windshield. Dancing Girl Tie pulled the car over to the curb and stopped.

"Should we take him to the station and grill him?"

I looked over at Yellow Tie. He pulled out his gun, checked it over carefully, opened the glove compartment and placed it inside. He opened the car door and stepped out.

"Benjamin, we don't want to ever see you again!"

I got out of the car and onto the sidewalk in front of my house. My mother was standing at the door with her arms crossed. As the car drove away, she rushed up, put her arms around me and hugged me.

"I'm so glad you're safe. Where were you?"

"I fell asleep in Eaton's."

She kneeled down in front of me on the sidewalk.

"Why aren't you going to school?"

"Don't know."

"I'm worried about you, you know," she squeezed my hands. "I'll tell you what, we'll go to school together tomorrow. Okay?"

"Okay." I gently put my sore hands in my pockets.

The next morning my mother dropped me off at the principal's office. In the classroom, Sister Anne was at her desk barking out the marks of our spelling lesson. When she got to my name I could feel myself shake with fright.

"Benjamin Flicker. It seems your days away from class have not helped your ability to spell. Twelve out of twenty wrong." She bent the long thin pointer in her hand. "Come up here!"

I left my seat and went to the head of the class.

"I'm trying." My throat was dry.

She shouted at the ceiling.

"There is no 'U' in forever! Alice, please count." She laid her pointer across the tips of my fingers.

"I don't want to."

"Count!"

Alice Aprile Abby sat at the desk in front of me. I hated for her to see the tears beginning to form in the corner of my eyes. I stared deep into Alice's blue eyes as tears began to fall down her cheeks.

"Twelve!" She turned quickly away.

"You may return to your seat, Benjamin," Sister Anne pushed me along with her hand on the back of my head.

"Can I go to the bathroom? I'm sorry. May I go?"

"Yes, you may."

I rushed to the door.

"And hurry back."

I went out the classroom door, down the hall, out the front doors and ran as fast as I could down the street, never looking back. Tears streamed down my face as I ran. I never went back to school that day. I didn't go home that night. It was June and it wasn't that cold, so I slept on the dirt under a balcony on Park Avenue.

I woke up hungry. I hadn't eaten since the Pepsi and the Mae

West I had late the afternoon before. I made my way back home, quietly walked up the back stairs of my house and opened the kitchen door. It was 5:30 a.m. No one was up. I went to the breadbox and, as quietly as I could, got the bread out. I placed two slices in the toaster and got out the butter and brown sugar.

I was standing by the toaster waiting for my bread when I heard a voice behind me.

"Your toast is done."

I turned. Will was there leaning against the doorway. I flipped down the sides of the toaster.

"Did you go to school yesterday?"

"Yes," I buttered my toast fast.

"Were you there all day?"

"Yes."

He walked toward me and with one swift move punched me right on the nose. I fell back, my eyes closed tightly as my bum hit the floor. My mind went blank. The next thing I heard was the butter knife hitting the floor beside my head.

"Don't lie to me. Don't ever lie to me!"

"I tried, Will! I really did!"

"Not good enough, Ben. Not good enough. You've got to stay in school." He stretched out his hand. "I'm sorry I hit you, kid."

"Is my nose bleeding?"

"Here, wipe it on my sleeve."

My nose left a trail of blood on the sleeve of his pajamas. He grabbed my hands to pull me to my feet and I cried out. He turned my hands over and angrily stared into my red, raw palms.

"Uh huh, uh huh," His head shook up and down over and over again. Then he looked me in the eye. "You go to school today. If I find out you didn't go, a little bloody nose will be the least of your worries. "

"Okay!"

"Good." He gently cupped my face in his hands. "We'll see if we can do something about this hand thing. Now go, go wash your face."

That afternoon I was in my class, trembling in my seat, waiting for the results of the spelling test when the door opened and there in the doorway … stood Will.

"You Sister Anne?"

"Yes. And who might you be?"

"I'm Benjamin's brother, Will. Is this the pointer you've been beating my brother with?"

He grabbed the pointer from her and slapped the top of her desk!

"I'll only say this once, Sister. If my brother ever comes home again with welts on his hands because of a beating he's gotten from you, for whatever reason, I will come back here and you will regret the day you ever took the habit. I guarantee God will punish you. Do you understand me, Sister?"

Sister Anne was as still as a lamppost.

Will took the pointer between his knuckles and snapped it in half.

Two seats away, George McGee, dirty-face George, his mouth was open so wide open I could've fit my fist in it.

"My brother will not be beaten by anyone and that includes you. If he needs a licking, I'll be the one who will give it to him. You will never lay a finger on my brother again!"

He walked over to the blackboard and picked up the bunch of pointers lying on the chalk holder.

"My brother loves cake! Did you know that, Sister? Chocolate cake! But if he can't hold a fork to eat his cake because of your way of teaching then I'd rather my brother eat cake than be taught by you," and he broke all the pointers over his knee. Pieces of wood covered the floor. My eyes were as big as saucers. Will stopped at the door and looked back.

"All I can say is this, Sister. Don't get on the wrong side of God." He pointed to his chest. "Today."

Alice Abby turned around in her seat, put her head in her hands, rested her elbows on my desk, leaned in close and said, "Oh Ben, I wish I had a brother."

The Egg-Salad Sandwich

ON THE MORNING OF NOVEMBER 8TH, 1953, I opened the large oak doors to St. Mike's Grade School in The Edge. I was being transferred from St. Luke's because of my bad attitude. I thought I was tough. Heck, most kids in this fifth-grade class had battle scars of some sort, either a black eye or a face full of cuts and bruises. When I came in the door it looked like a big fight had just happened. Everyone was staring at the open window where a boy had a tight grip on a pair of legs. I could only see the white and black running shoes held high over his shoulders. The kid outside the window was screaming.

The kid inside was laughing.

"Please, don't let me go!" the upside-down kid screamed.

"Oh shit! My hand is slipping!" the inside kid laughed back.

"Tom Kennedy! Bring that boy back in here." Sister Teresa bristled as she entered and slammed her books on her desk. "And stop swearing!"

"Yes, Sister," Tom Kennedy replied politely in his Irish voice.

"And close the window! It's freezing in here," she ordered.

Then, as if he was doing some good deed, he gently brought the upside-down kid back into the room. "Hey, Dennis, what the heck you doing out there? You could kill yourself. Come on, let me help you back in here!"

That's where I first met Dennis Tallman. I guess the reason they picked on Dennis was because his parents were separated. His father had left him and his mum for another woman. They tried to keep it quiet because his dad still lived in The Edge, but I guess that didn't work. Everybody knew.

A few weeks later Dennis and I were confined together in the cloakroom. We were at opposite ends of the rectangular room with our faces stuck in the corners. The nuns who taught us, The Congregation of Notre Dame, CND for short, would most times make us stay in the classroom and hold sheets of paper against the blackboard with our noses. But this particular day Sister Teresa had had enough and wanted us out of her sight completely, hence the cloakroom.

"It stinks in here!" Dennis whispered across the room.

"Yeah," I said in return.

"What is that shitty smell?" he said with disgust.

"Wool," I replied. "Wet wool, I smell it all the time."

We remained quiet for some time, consuming the rich odour of our surroundings, trying our best not to break the code of silence. If they heard us in the classroom, then we'd have to remain there all day. I was doing fine, but Dennis just couldn't keep quiet.

"I can't stand this smell!" Dennis whined.

"Shut up, will ya! I don't want to stay here all day."

"I think I'm going to be sick!" he said.

"Are you gonna puke?" I asked.

"Yeah! I think so."

"Well, puke in your corner, okay?" I replied.

"Why?" he asked.

"Cuz I don't want to look at it," I said.

"Oh, shit, I'm gonna be sick, I can feel it!"

I turned my head out of the corner, and there he was, moving around the cloakroom as if he was looking for a place to hide, his hand over his mouth making moaning sounds.

"Oh shit, oh no, oh no!" And finally he blurted out, "I'm gonna be sick!!!!"

He opened the pocket of some kids coat that was hanging on a hook on the wall and puked in it. He stopped and slid down the wall and sat on the floor.

"I'll get Sister Teresa," I said getting up.

"No, no, no…. I'm okay," he said.

"Are you sure?" I asked.

"Yeah, I'm fine. I'm fine now," he responded quietly.

I went over and sat down next to him on the floor.

"That was really something. You puked in someone's coat pocket!"

"Well, it's your fault."

"How come?" I asked.

"Because you told me you didn't want to look at it," he smiled back.

"Man, you puked in somebody's pocket!"

"Yeah," he grinned.

We looked at each other and we both began to laugh. Dennis pressed his finger to his lips.

"Keep it down. Sister Teresa's got ears like an elephant!"

We got control of ourselves and quietly sat there staring at all the winter coats on the other side of the room.

Finally, Dennis spoke up.

"Hey, I hear your father's dead."

"Yeah," I said quietly.

"When did he die?" he asked.

"Oh, when I was five." I answered. "Why?"

"It's Christmas and I always think of my dad at Christmas," he said, lowering his eyes to the floor.

"Well, I got a lot of brothers and sisters. I guess I really don't need a dad," I lied.

"Oh yeah. Everybody needs a dad," he mumbled back.

"Well, I don't really remember him, you know." I lied again.

"I wish I could forget my dad," he responded. "There are times I'd like to kill him!"

"What good would that do?"

Dennis paused and thought a bit, and then said,

"At least he'd be outta the neighbourhood."

My attention was taken to the sound of water.

"What's that dripping?" I asked.

We both looked in the direction of the coat with the puke in it and then to each other.

"Whose coat is that anyway?" I asked.

Dennis smiled a crazy grin and said, "Tom Kennedy's!"

There was an incredible look of satisfaction on his face as he grinned back at me.

"What'd you puke in there?" I said, not really wanting to know the answer.

"Egg-salad sandwiches!" He stuck his tongue out and his eyes got big. "I can hardly wait!"

Later that same day the school called Dennis's dad to come and talk to them and see if he could help straighten his son out. Dennis was really nervous about his dad coming.

"Hey, Ben!" he shouted. He came running up to me and was very much out of breath. "Hey, Ben, do you … ah … think you could stick around for a while?" he asked, snapping his fingers rapidly by his side.

"Why? What for? You got a detention or something?" I asked.

"Nah…. It's just that I want you to stick around."

"But why?" I insisted.

He said nothing but just stared back at me and then looked

away as if he wanted to say something but couldn't.

"I gotta go...."

"My dad's coming!" he said. "My real dad's coming and I just don't want to be … alone." His voice got quiet. "That's all."

But before I could respond the doors opened at the far end of the hall. Dennis's dad stepped through the doorway. He was a short, thin, wiry man. Slowly he started to walk toward us.

"Hey, I gotta go," I said quickly.

"No, stay!" he gripped my arm. "Please wait for me! Wait for me right here! Please!" he pleaded.

I nodded yes and he walked away to meet his father half way down the hallway. They stopped and looked at each other for a long time and then as his father reached out to touch him. Dennis backed away up against the metal lockers.

"I hate you!" Dennis shouted.

"I don't hate you," his father said, trying to comfort him.

"Well, I hate you!" Dennis's voice was almost inaudible. His head dropped to his chest as he stared at the hallway floor.

"Okay. You hate me. But I'm still your father. And I want you to stop fuckin' around here. Do what you're told!" His father was determined to get his point across.

"I hear you puked in some kid's coat pocket?" he asked.

Dennis said nothing.

"Well, did you or didn't you puke in some kid's pocket?" His voice cut through the air.

Still there was no reply.

"Well, did you?" His voice echoed down the hallway.

"So what! You left us! I don't need you here!" Dennis's eyes were glued to the hallway floor.

His father reached out and cuffed Dennis on the side of his head. The blow was so hard that it knocked Dennis down onto the floor.

"Get up! Come on, get up!" Dennis didn't move.

"I said get up!" he yelled, kicking him on the side of his bum.

Dennis jumped quickly to his feet and began to run toward me.

"Come on, Ben. Let's get outta here," he yelled as he passed.

We burst through the big heavy doors at the far end of the hallway and ran across the schoolyard. We stopped at the fence that bordered Cursoll Street.

"Are you okay?" I looked at Dennis.

Dennis, trying to catch his breath, looked back. There was an incredible determination in his eyes.

"He didn't hurt me. Yeah, he didn't hurt me at all."

A sad smile appeared at the corners of his mouth. He turned. And he began to run.

Friends Forever

I SAT IN THE BACK OF DOUG LEMONS's '48 Chevy with my best friends, Dennis, Steven and Slick, heading down the highway. Elvis was belting out "Blue Suede Shoes" on the radio. We sang at the top of our lungs because we were so happy that Doug, who was our Big Brother at the downtown community centre, arranged this fishing trip. We all thought he was crazy. A fishing trip! Heck, the closest any of us got to the country was when we sat on the benches at Trenholm Park at the corner of my street.

The five of us piled out of the old '48 Chevy and got our gear out of the trunk. You would have thought that fishing gear was important to us when we packed our bags. But, no. We had other things on our minds.

Dennis Tallman's overnight bag had of one small box of Eddy matches, an extra pair of underwear and a bodybuilding magazine with pictures showing how to get bigger muscles.

Dennis had told me that girls liked guys with muscles, so I brought my brother's two ten-pound dumbbells. I didn't own any fishing gear.

Steven 'Lockjaw' Keifer's bag was full of food. His mother once said she wished he'd get lockjaw just so he'd lose some weight and the name stuck. Lockjaw was 205 pounds and 5'5". We were

scared to touch his overnighter for fear he would sit on us and crush us to death! No fishing gear.

Dirty-face George McGee hated his first name so he called himself Slick, because he said it was sexy. He brought no bag. Slick was dressed in his usual black Wellingtons, jeans, a spotless white teeshirt and a denim jacket. He had a thick, black, greased-backed Elvis hairdo. No fishing gear. He did have his comb, though, because you never knew when a wind would come up. He also carried a clarinet. Two years of classes and Slick couldn't play a lick on that thing.

Our leader, Doug Lemons, was seventeen. Doug was born with one leg shorter than the other, yet when we played tackle football he'd be the toughest guy on the field. When he got the ball all you'd see were arms, legs and shoulders flying in different directions. But every time we hit him, he'd crumble. You thought he was dead, but he'd jump up, ready to go again. Crazy! I always wondered if being crippled had anything to do with that.

It was a two-mile boat ride from the mainland to our small fishing camp on the island. This made me nervous because I had a fear of water. I can only blame it on my mother. She never learned to swim and never encouraged me to. My tensed hands clutched the bottom of my seat as I stared at the water splashing against the sides of the cramped little motorboat.

When we arrived, Dennis and I put up a tent that had spikes that we hammered into the ground using large stones. Slick combed his hair and gave us advice. Thanks to Dennis's box of Eddy matches, a fire was lit and thanks to Doug, fish lay in the frying pan, their heads still on.

"Why are their eyes so slimy?" I asked.

"Their slimy eyes are the best part," Lockjaw said.

"Do you have to keep saying 'slimy'?" Slick piped in.

Doug laid the frying pan on the open fire.

"I know an Indian legend about that," Lockjaw said. "One night, an Indian kid named Two Moon Eyes sat beside a camp fire with his mother and father."

"This isn't a ghost story, is it?" Slick sat upright. "I can't stand ghost stories. Hey, not that I'm scared, cuz I'm not." His comb glided through his Elvis hair.

"It's a legend!" Dennis said, rolling up his magazine.

Slick placed his clarinet to his lips. We all stared at him in silence. We all knew he couldn't play, yet he pretended he could.

"The girls love it when I play this thing! They squeal." I must admit that he did look good holding it.

"When? After they leave?" Dennis snickered.

"No … but if that's the way you guys feel…." He slowly placed the clarinet down against the stump he was sitting on. He pointed at Lockjaw.

"If this is a ghost story…." He shook his finger, "I'm just sayin'."

"Right." Lockjaw smiled back. "So anyway, Two Moon Eyes and his folks were sitting round the fire and his dad said, 'Go down to the river and fill this bucket.' It was dark and Two Moon Eyes being only eight was scared to go alone, but his dad said, 'Don't be frightened. The distance is short. Go!' What his dad didn't know was that someone or something was watching them from the woods and Two Moon Eyes had to walk by them to get to the river."

Lockjaw ate a handful of jujubes.

"This is stupid!" Slick said.

"Come on, Slick, just let him finish!" I gasped, trying to lift a dumbbell.

"It's stupid, really stupid," Slick muttered, sitting down on a large stump.

"So Two Moon Eyes started down toward the river," Lockjaw whispered. "As he walked he thought he heard noises. He stopped. He looked around. Listened. Nothing, so he started off again. But the eyes in the woods followed him."

"What eyes?" Slick shouted, standing up.

"Two Moon Eyes got to the river bank," Lockjaw's voice was getting more hushed, "and as he put the bucket down he heard it. He froze! It was a noise. Oh yeah, he heard footsteps coming closer, closer! He looked right, then left.... Nothing! He got down onto the riverbank, kneeled, and just as he was about to scoop the water into the bucket, he looked into the river and saw reflected just above his own head, the head of someone else!"

"So what! So what!" Slick paced around the fire.

"The Face had no eyes!" Lockjaw screamed back.

"Stupid ... stupid ... stupid, stupid, stupid. I'm not listening! I'm not," Slick muttered, combing his hair. "The guy had no eyes? Oh ... oh, well, maybe his eyes were closed!"

"No way, man," Lockjaw shot back. "He had no eyelids, just two empty ... black ... holes."

"Ah, geez." Slick sat down.

"'I want your golden eyes!' He put his hand on Two Moon Eyes's shoulder so Two Moon Eyes closed his eyes as tight as he could. The Face's grip was so strong that it spun him round on the spot. 'Look deep into my black heart!' Two Moon Eyes didn't want to open his eyes, but he couldn't help himself. He could feel the Face's fingernails on his eyelids. He had to take a peek...."

"Oh, right. He has to peek," Slick shouted, his fingers buried in his hair.

"He ever-so-gently squeezed his eyes open and peeked through his eyelashes. The Face was ten feet tall! And his whole body was covered with eyes ... eyes the Face already collected from other people."

"You're nuts!" Slick said, shutting his eyes and placing his hands over his ears. "I am not listening."

Lockjaw began to move around the perimeter of our campfire as he continued. "'I want your golden eyes!' The voice shook the ground around Two Moon Eyes. As the Face moved in closer, Two Moon Eyes jumped up, screamed and ran as fast as he could. He looked over his shoulder. The Face, flying through the trees, opened its cape and thousands of eyes escaped into the woods. The Face yelled, 'I want your golden eyes!'

"When Two Moon Eyes reached his campfire his folks were gone.

"'HELP! HELP!' he screamed. Then he heard the sizzling sounds from the frying pan on the fire. He saw the eyes of two beautiful perch looking back at him. Two Moon Eyes quickly took the pan off the fire, got a fork and plucked the slimy eyes from the fish. He had them in his hand! Two golden eyes! 'I want your golden eyes,' cried the Face from the woods. Two Moon Eyes closed his eyes and placed one slimy fish eye on each eyelid. He could hear the Face coming up behind him."

As Lockjaw circled us, he stopped and stood behind Slick.

"When he felt the Face almost on top of him, he turned quickly to face the Face and as he did the Face's two, big, floating hands scooped down....

"I GOT 'EM," Lockjaw yelled, putting his fingers on Slick's eyelids.

Slick jumped off the old log so fast he hit Lockjaw in the chin with his head and knocked him out cold. His scream echoed through the forest out onto the lake and came back to us at least six times. Lockjaw couldn't chew for an hour.

That night, lying in our sleeping bags, we laughed and promised to be friends forever.

Best Two Weeks of My Life

It was a beautiful early summer day. I was at the park with Lockjaw, Dennis and Slick playing four-man baseball. Baseball was one of my passions. My dad would take me to see the Montreal Royals play down at De Lorimier Stadium. He would tell me about the history of the team from when they started in 1870 to the time when Jackie Robinson played for them. I was hooked on baseball. My dream was that one day I would be the first and only professional baseball player from my neighbourhood to play in the major leagues.

Steven and Dennis were in the outfield and Slick was pitching. I was at home plate with the bat in my hands waiting for the next pitch. I looked out at the pitcher's mound and Slick. He was winding up and ready to throw. As he was about to throw the ball, I saw out of the corner of my eye Alice Abby riding her bike near the stands. Her red hair was tied up in a ponytail. Alice's bike was a CCM girl's Classic Hollywood. The frame was painted deep pink with dark purple stripes on white fenders. It had big white-wall balloon tires, a large headlight on the handlebars and a chrome bell near the right-hand grip.

She got off her bike and took it over and leaned it against the bleacher seats. Her ponytail bounced on her shoulders as she climbed and sat on the bench, fourth row up.

I saw the pitch from Slick too late, swung my bat furiously at the ball, and missed.

"Okay, you're done. Strike three!" Lockjaw shouted from the outfield.

Alice looked at me and smiled. I shrugged and smiled back.

"No. No … foul tip!" Slick yelled out to Lockjaw.

Dennis threw his glove on the ground with great gusto. "Oh, come on, Slick! He's out!"

"I'm up!" Lockjaw started running toward the infield.

"Stay there!" Slick shouted back, "Let's give him one more! Pay attention, Ben. This is going to be a good one!"

Slick quickly pitched one more ball and I belted it high into the air toward Dennis. He tried to catch it but didn't have his glove on and the ball flew past him. In four-man baseball all you had to do was run to first and back to home again before the ball got there. I ran to first base as fast as I could and rushed to get back to home plate where Slick was waiting for me. "Nice swing, man. You got a piece of that!"

As I crossed the plate I looked over to where Alice was sitting but she was no longer there.

"I gotta go. Sorry guys." I grabbed my glove.

"Where ya going?" Dennis asked as he picked up the bat.

"I gotta go try and talk my mum into not making me go to camp!" I jumped on my blue Schwinn and headed across the grass toward home.

The spokes on the front wheel of my bike were spinning at rapid speed. I bounced over the uneven ground. My legs were desperately trying to catch up with the pedals as they spun effortlessly beneath the crossbar. I was late and my mother was waiting.

I raced toward the park swimming pool and the large green bathhouse. As I turned the far corner of the building Alice was

kneeling on the ground looking sadly at the wheel of her bike. Her front tire was flat as a pancake. I jammed on my breaks. My back wheel skidded out from under me, dirt flew into the air and I stopped on a dime.

"Hi." With my eyes open wide the words slipped off my lips. "You okay?"

"Hi, Ben." she looked up at me. "I got a flat." She pointed down at the front tire. She said it so easily.

"You got a repair kit?"

"A what?"

I got off my bike and rested it against the bathhouse wall. Alice shrugged her shoulders.

"Never mind. I do." I opened the small leather pouch hanging from the back of my seat. I took out a wrench, a patch and a small tube of glue. I removed the air pump from my bike and placed it on ground.

"Can you fix it?"

"Sure."

"You got time? You were really riding fast like you were in a hurry to get somewhere." Her voice was so soft it seemed to hang on the air like an echo. I turned the bike upside down and started to remove the front wheel. She smiled at me.

The thought of my mother waiting drifted far from my mind. "Yeah, I got lots of time."

"It's hard to walk a bike with a flat tire," she said, biting her lip. "I was going to Christie's to get a sundae and it just went flat."

"You've got a tack in the tire."

"Where?" She leaned down. Her face was next to mine, almost touching. I could feel my heart beating faster. I removed the inner tube, spat, rubbed the spot with my fingers and showed her the small hole.

"Oh my God! You spat on my tire!"

"Sorry 'bout that. Only way to get the dirt off and make the glue stick, but don't worry, you're never gonna see it."

She stood up. "I was watching you play baseball." She took my glove off my handlebars and put it on.

"I'm not very good."

"I like baseball." She spread out the fingers of the glove.

"Yeah? I play in the park league."

"I know," she pounded her fist into the mitt, "Thursday nights."

My heart stopped. She knew I played baseball Thursday nights! I looked into her eyes. I was speechless and the only words I could think of were, "It's done!"

"Thanks, Ben." She leaned down, her face, next to mine again.

"That's okay." I turned toward her and my nose brushed the side of her cheek.

"Holy cow!" She smiled.

When I got home I could hear the piano being played in the parlour. My mum was sitting at the well-worn upright against the living room wall. My mum loved singing. On Friday nights she'd sing down at the old Dominion. Frankie liked singing too and I went with him once to hear her. She was great.

I came into the living room and sat down beside her on the piano bench.

"Sorry I'm late." I threw my mitt in the corner.

Her fingers tripped along the piano keys. "The garbage has to be put out, and did you pick up the chicken from the butcher?"

"Oh, no. I thought Frankie was going to do that."

"No, I asked you to do it."

"Why do I have to do everything? How come he never does anything? Get out the garbage, go to the store and dry the dishes! Is it cuz he's sixteen?"

She stopped playing for a moment and looked over at me. She gently placed her hand on my face. "I can depend on you, Ben. All I got is you." She cupped my face in her hands and kissed my nose. The same nose that brushed Alice's cheek.

"I'll go get the chicken. I'll put out the garbage. I'll dry the dishes but after doing all that can I get out of going to camp this year?"

She grabbed my nose between her fingers, "Oh, you are so cute."

"Mum, you know I've been going to camp since I was five."

"Uh huh."

"I'm thirteen."

"Not quite," she interrupted and went back to playing the piano.

"Okay, but in a couple of months."

"Stop trying to grow up so fast. You got your whole life to do that. And pick up your mitt. Put it in your room."

"Why do I have to go?" I whined.

"Because you gotta do what you gotta do!" She pinged one of

the keys on the piano and lifted her hand into the air.

"Mum!"

"You gotta go. That's final." My head sank to my chest. My breathing became heavy.

She stopped playing and put her arm around my shoulder. "You'll be with me, working the kitchen. Just the two of us."

"I'll miss my friends."

"I'd miss you," she kissed me on the side of my cheek. "Do you wanna play a song together?" She ran her fingers along the keys.

"No," I said sadly, "not now."

I got up, grabbed my mitt from the corner and took it into my room. I fell back onto my bed and stared at the ceiling. The last thing I remember before I fell asleep was the smile on Alice Abby's face as my nose brushed the side her cheek.

When I woke up I made myself a toasted sandwich of peanut butter and molasses on dark rye. Then I walked down the lane toward the bottom of my street where, just below the train tracks, there is an open field with a small creek that runs down into the river.

The grass stood high and uncut along the tracks. Down at the water's edge wildflowers were blooming. The late morning sun glistened off the water. I could hear voices and the sound of glass breaking. Dennis and Slick were throwing stones at old bottles and tin cans. Lockjaw was sitting against the bank eating jujubes out of a paper bag.

"You see that? I broke that bottle!" Dennis shouted. "One shot! Did ya see it?"

Lockjaw jumped up. "No shit! Bingo!"

Dennis and Lockjaw jumped over the creek to inspect the damage.

"So, did ya get out of it?" Slick tossed the stone in his hand to the ground.

"I have to go."

"You could run away."

"I don't think so."

"Yeah, you could. That would be cool. You could stay at my house," Lockjaw shouted at us as he crossed back over the creek.

"Your mother would tell."

Dennis tried to jump over but his foot landed in the water.

"Shit!" He pulled his wet dripping shoe out of the creek.

"She hardly ever comes into my room. Hey, Ben, you could tell her you're sick … at the last minute."

"That would be a lie. I can't lie to my mother."

"Yeah, but you could fix it later and tell her you got better!" Lockjaw smiled back.

"Look at this, my sock is soaking wet!" Dennis said holding up his dripping sock.

"Tough luck," Lockjaw laughed.

I moved over and sat on the bank, thinking of my camping predicament.

"Saw you with Alice yesterday," Slick whispered, joining me on the ground.

"I was fixing her bike. Flat tire."

"Alice is cute. I think she likes you."

"Why do you say that?"

"Just saying," Slick winked.

"Come on, Lockjaw, let's go down to the creek. Catch some frogs."

"Hey Den, you ever eat them?"

"It's a miracle he's still alive cause he eats everything," Slick laughed.

I watched them go down to the water, thinking of what Slick had just said to me about Alice. And once again her soft cheek came into my mind.

"Listen, I'll see you guys later. I gotta go," I said. I headed home to try to think of another way out.

I was sitting on the steps out in the back yard with Frankie, trying my best to convince him to help me with my camp problem.

Sometimes talking to my older brother Frankie was the most difficult thing in the world, though. He would look at me, seem to be listening, but nothing would really get through.

"You could tell Mum you'll look after me!"

"Can't do that, Ben. Got stuff to do." He brushed some lint off his shirt, a toothpick hanging on his lower lip.

"You don't have to take care of me, I can do that!" I begged.

"What if Will finds out, huh? And he tells Mum, huh? She finds out I lied to her, huh? Then she beats the crap out of me." He shrugged his shoulders.

"She can't do that!"

"Oh, yes she can. Our mum is tough! Tougher than Will."

"I'm dead."

"You're not dead. You're just going to camp."

We both sat not saying a word. Frankie bent down, un-did his shoe laces and tied them back up again. He kept doing it over and over again until he seemed satisfied with the bow. I watched his fingers move at rapid speed working his laces until perfection was achieved. Finally, I looked up at my brother.

"Frankie." I stopped for a moment, not knowing if it was safe to continue. "What's being in love like?"

Frankie completed his final bow and began to chuckle, "What? Are you in love?"

"No!"

"Who is she?"

"Nobody."

"Yeah? Well, it's not like anything else. I can tell ya that."

"Don't ya know?"

"Nobody knows, kid. Is it that Alice girl from school? I hear you're fixin' her bike and stuff."

I avoided his eyes and looked out into the back yard.

"I don't wanna go to camp this year."

Frankie grabbed my shoulder and turned me toward him.

"It's Alice!" he smiled.

"No...." I turned away.

"It is! It's Alice!" Frankie got up quickly and stood in front of me. "Am I right?"

I got up and moved past him but my feet got locked in place as Frankie tackled me to the ground. He sat on top of me, pinning me down.

"I'm right! Tell me I'm right!"

"No!" I struggled to get free. We were like an octopus, arms and legs flying in every direction. I finally squirmed out from under him, and once I did I ran out the back-yard gate, down the alley into Canal Street.

The next morning the rain was pounding against the windows of St. Anthony's Church. It was Sunday and I'd just finished serving the nine am Mass. Father Mac was hanging up his robe in the mahogany closet along the mahogany wall in the vestibule.

"You were late with the wine today."

"Sorry 'bout that, Father."

"One thing you can't be late with is the wine."

"Won't happen again, Father." I stood staring at the hook on the wall.

"Something on your mind, Ben?"

He closed the closet door. The door didn't click when it closed; it had a swish sound. It was almost silent.

"Father, if someone tells a lie but they can fix it later, is it still a lie?" I hung my gown on the hanger and placed it on the hook on the wall.

"Is this someone you know?"

"Yeah, he's a friend. I mean, I don't know him that well."

He came closer and put his hand on my shoulder.

"Pass me the boot polish. It's in the box in the closet."

I opened the closet where his robe was hanging, got the box and brought it to him. He sat down in the big, overstuffed armchair in front of me.

"Give my shoe a wipe with the boot rag."

"Yes, Father." I took the rag and wiped the dust from his shoe.

“A lie is a lie no matter how big or small. Whether you fix it later or not.”

“I’ll tell him.” I returned the rag, got up, put the box back in the closet.

“Aren’t you going to camp tomorrow?”

“Yes, Father.”

“Have you got a replacement for Mass next week?”

“No, Father,” I closed the silent door of the closet.

“Well, you need to get someone.” He put his arm on my shoulder and walked me to street door. “It’s important. I depend on you. Can’t do it without you.” He looked down at me, “What are you smiling about?”

“Oh, nothing, Father. You’re right. I’m important. I’ll let my mother know.”

With that I went out of the church into the pouring rain.

My mother was folding my clothes and packing them into my suitcase very efficiently, just as I had seen her adding ingredients when making a cake.

"Underwear on the bottom, socks tucked in the corner, now tee-shirts nicely folded, and pants right on top," she said, gently pushing the socks into the corner of the suitcase. "When you unpack and put things away, they go in the drawer the opposite way. First the pants, then the tee-shirts…." She stopped and looked over at me.

"Nicely folded," I nodded.

"Good. The socks and last but not least, the underwear, first to go in and last to come out. They sit on top of the pile in your drawer, to remind you to change them, often."

I folded the blue tee-shirt on the bed carefully, knowing my mother's eyes were on me like a sniper.

"Father Mac says I'm important. He depends on me." She read my mind. That's about all I could get out before she turned and shouted. "Frankie!"

"Not Frankie, Mum!"

"He's served hundreds of Masses." She dismissed the thought, as if it were nothing, with the wave of her hand.

"Yeah, what's up?" Frankie said, sticking his head in the room.

"I want you to take Ben's place and serve Mass next Sunday."

"Why is it, any time you shout my name, you want me to do something!"

"Do you know when to serve the wine? He really gets peeved if you don't get it to him on time," I threatened.

"You hear that! A priest threatens you if you don't get him his booze on time!"

"You're going to serve Mass for him and that's that. Brush up on the service. It's still in Latin."

"I'll be the oldest altar boy in history!" His head disappeared.

“You’ll get over it!” my mother shouted, as the door banged shut. Not at all like the mahogany doors in the church’s vestibule.

The rain had turned into a light drizzle as I walked dejectedly down Elmhurst Avenue. I turned down the laneway leading to Slick’s house, stopped at the window of his bedroom and knocked on the glass. Slick opened the window and I crawled inside. The room was dimly lit. It was the way Slick liked it. I looked around and finally sat down on the edge of his bed.

“I’ve tried everything. I’m going to camp.” I put my head in my hands.

“Isn’t it on a lake? You get to go swimming, fishing.... Heck, they feed ya, don’t they? What am I sayin’! You’re workin’ in the kitchen!”

I looked up at Slick sitting on the windowsill. “Yeah, they feed ya,” I assured him.

“You get to eat all day. What’s wrong with that!”

“So, couldn’t get out of it, huh?” Lockjaw laughed, appearing at the window with Dennis.

“Wish I was goin’ to camp. Sounds cool,” Dennis said dejectedly.

Slick looked at Lockjaw, “They feed him three squares a day!”

“I’d go!”

Dennis slapped him on the side of the head. “We all know you’d go, if there was food.”

“Hey, stop that! You could shake his brains loose!”

“Hey, Slick, very funny! Ha, ha,” Lockjaw looked over at me on the bed. “What kinda stuff you do at this camp?”

“Help my mum in the kitchen.”

“Cooking?” Lockjaw’s eyes lit up. “My mum won’t even let me in the kitchen.”

“Anything crazy ever happen there?” Dennis pushed his head through the open window.

“Once there was this guy whose mum was one of the cooks and he sneaked into the pantry where they kept sacks of flour, potatoes and brown sugar, stuff like that. Big sacks of it! And he stayed in there all day and night and he ate, like, half a sack of brown sugar."

"Cool," Lockjaw said, trying to get in the window with Dennis.

"Only you would think that's cool." Slick flicked Lockjaw on the head with his finger.

"Oops, I think I heard your brains move!"

"He must have been sick!" Dennis scrunched up his face.

"No. He was just crazy!" I lamented.

My mother was sitting on the bus at the front next to fellow camp worker, Estelle Monahan. The two women were talking at a furious clip. I could hear my mother's voice, loud and clear.

"As soon as we get there, Estelle, we've got to lock up that pantry. Look." She produced something from her pocket. "Padlock!"

I was sitting on the bus on my own trying to save an empty seat beside me so it would be a comfortable ride to the country.

Slick, Lockjaw and Dennis were standing on the sidewalk with their baseball gear. They leaned against their bikes waving goodbye. I sat there, my head resting against the cool glass of the window. I looked out and Slick was waving at me. I waved back. But his wave was more insistent. I tried to open the window but it was stuck. Slick began to wave like a crazy man, pointing toward the front door of the bus. Finally, I looked in the direction we were pointed. It was jammed with kids still getting on. I looked out at Slick again and he was still waving frantically, pointing at the front. I stood up, looked down the aisle.

Suddenly, I saw Alice Abby. She was dressed in a pair of blue jeans, sneakers and a striped tee-shirt. Her long red hair was tied with a bow at the back of her head. She looked incredible! She was walking down the aisle toward the empty seat beside me. I looked out the window and Slick was smiling and giving me the thumbs up.

"Anybody sitting here?" Her voice was so soft that it cut out all the other noise on the bus. I couldn't hear any other voice but hers.

"Uh … nope."

She lifted her small bag to put it above in the storage rack.

"I can do that."

"Thanks." A smile came to her face. That same smile I kept seeing every time I closed my eyes.

"You want to sit by the window?"

"Oh no, that's your seat."

"That's okay, I know this road like the back of my hand."

"Great. Then we won't get lost." She giggled as she slid past me to the window seat.

The bus jerked away and I fell back into the seat beside her. I looked over her shoulder out the window at Slick who was throwing his hands in the air and dancing some kind of crazy dance on the sidewalk.

"This is my first time going to camp," Alice said with a slight waver in her voice.

"It's fun. You'll have a great time," I reassured her.

Alice looked in my eyes. "Good."

The bus pulled away from the community centre's front doors.

"You can depend on me," I said quietly, never taking my eyes off her. It felt so good to stare into her eyes.

"I'll hold you to it," she said, as if there was nothing else to be said. She smiled.

My heart was beating really fast. Was this the feeling that Frankie couldn't explain?

The Paper Route

WE WERE ALL TOLD TO SHOW UP at Slick's around seven because Dennis had some news for us all. I was a little late making my way up Waverly Street through the day's heavy snowfall. This was just another winter blizzard in Montreal. There were usually four a year and when you reached the fourth one you felt that spring was just around the corner. This was blizzard number two so I walked up Waverly with a heavy heart. Slick lived over on Westmore Avenue, ground floor, Apartment 1.

His bedroom was in the back of the apartment that he shared with various members of his clan. When I opened the door all the guys looked over at me. Lockjaw was sitting on the side of Slick's bed with an open bag of jujubes on his lap. Dennis was beside him, busy counting out a handful of change from his pocket and Slick was leaning up against the frame of his bedroom window. A Player's Navy Cut cigarette hung from his lip.

"What's up?"

"What the hell took you so long?" Dennis shouted at me as I stood in the doorway.

"Sorry 'bout that, guys. My mother couldn't get my sister Winn out from under the bed so I had to finish drying the dinner dishes."

"Okay, okay. So what's all the secrecy about?" Lockjaw whispered, chewing on some of the candy he took from the bag on his lap.

"Hey, Ben, do you mind?" Slick said, pointing to the open door.

"Right … right. I'll get it." I turned around and closed the bedroom door. Only the light from the laneway street light filtered through the window shade, and it created an eerie feel.

"Okay, Dennis, I haven't got all night," Slick insisted.

"Okay. Okay. But I don't want you guys to tell anyone about this," Dennis whispered back. He took a deep breath and let it out slowly. "This morning a friend…."

"Hold it," Slick interrupted. "If we're going to have to sit in the dark and listen to something about a friend when we all know that you're talking about yourself, because you don't have any other friends but us, I'm turning on the light."

"Okay, okay. It's me," Dennis whispered back.

"Thank you. We shall remain in darkness."

"But you can't tell anyone."

We all answered at once, "Right! Yeah, got it! How many times do ya have to ask?"

We all agreed that we would not utter a word. All but Slick. He dragged on his cigarette blowing the smoke out the bedroom window. He never uttered a word. Slick hated to commit to anything.

"This morning I was delivering my papers. I cut through the lane out back of 1836 Western, Apartment 2, and I saw it. I couldn't believe my eyes! I just stared through the window!"

"What? What did you see?" I leaned in.

"She was naked! In the buff with nipples showing and fleshy thighs, a bare ass…."

"That's disgusting," I uttered, backing away.

"I love these stories," Lockjaw whispered, practically choking on a mouth full of candy.

I looked over at Slick in the dark. The glow on the end of his cigarette got brighter as he took a deep drag. The light reflected off his white tee-shirt and gave him a glorious hue as he gently rested one of his black Wellington boots on the windowsill. He hooked his thumb into the belt loop of his jeans and rested his hand on his hip, fag and all.

"I think we'd better get him a glass of water," I said, hitting Lockjaw on the back.

"No, I'm okay," he said catching his breath. "What did you see?"

"First, I gotta tell ya, it was cold! You guys don't know how cold it is at 4:30 in the morning carrying newspapers. The tips of my fingers were numb. I could see my breath. I could feel the cold snow through the bottom of my snow boots."

"We don't need the weather report, for Christ sake!" Lockjaw jumped in.

"Yeah, get on with it. I gotta meet Doreen in the back of the Caddie in thirty minutes," Slick added casually.

"Doreen! I love Doreen! You just never stop!" I screamed out loud.

"No, you don't. I love Doreen. It'll be tonight."

"Who gives a shit about Doreen?" Lockjaw sounded like his patience had run out. "Ah, sorry Slick, but I would have to give you big bucks to hear what Doreen looks like in the buff. Dennis is givin' me this one for free! So let's get back to the weather report! Okay? Dennis, please continue! I'm all ears."

"So I'm standing there and she starts to move around the room. I could see her, clear as day. She is beautiful! I watched her as she walked across the room, then she disappeared. So I leaned in to see if I could find her naked body."

"This is disgustingly good," Lockjaw piped in.

"Only to you," Slick shot back, and he took another drag on his cigarette.

Lockjaw spit out the candy he had in his mouth into his hand.

"What'd you do?"

"I placed my bag of papers down on the ground and I noticed something peeking out of the snow. I took a closer look and guess what it was?"

"You could have been arrested as a peeping tom," I informed the gang.

"It was 4:30 in the morning!" Lockjaw answered back. "Who's going to see him?"

"That's when peeping toms do peeping tomming, stupid!"

"Will you keep it down! You'll get my mother in here," Slick shot back in the dark. "And you do not want to deal with her. Not tonight."

"Your dad?" I inquired.

"Yeah, lost his job."

"Sorry," I responded.

"He'll find another one," Slick said, ignoring me and trying to get back to the business at hand. "So, what the hell was it?"

"It was a two-dollar bill," Dennis said, making it sound like a million. "It was stuck in the snow! So I took off my gloves and began to dig. My fingers were freezing. I tried to pull it out but all I ended up with was this." Dennis reached into his pocket and pulled out half a two-dollar bill.

"Oh no!" I said dejectedly. "Was the other half buried somewhere nearby?"

"What happened to the beautiful naked woman in Apartment 2?" Lockjaw wanted to know.

"What a day, right? First to see the most beautiful naked woman I'd ever seen and to find half a two-dollar bill!"

"There we have it, fellows! His reward for all his hard work? Getting up early every morning for weeks and weeks, carrying hundreds of newspapers in a bag for miles through the snow, sleet, rain and sometimes sunshine and all he ends up with is a flash from some nude broad and half a two-dollar bill," Slick philosophized.

"Okay, so the money thing was a bad deal. But at least she was a good lookin' nude babe, right?" Lockjaw jumped in. "What happened to her?"

"So what are you gonna do?" I asked ignoring Lockjaw's naked woman fetish.

"I thought if you guys would come with me tomorrow morning and help me look for the other half of the money...." Dennis spoke sheepishly.

"And the lady in Apartment 2?" Lockjaw asked.

"She'll be there," Dennis replied. "She always is."

"I'm in." Lockjaw couldn't get the words out fast enough.

"You would be." I shot a disgusted look at him.

We all sat in the dark in silence for a few moments. Lockjaw stuffed his hand in his bag of candy and popped a jujube. Slick moved quietly, took a comb out of his back pocket and began to pull it through his thick black hair. As for me, even though I was disgusted at the thought of peeking in someone's window, I was painting a picture in my mind of that laneway behind 1836 Western Avenue, Apartment 2.

"So, you want to go, or what?" Dennis broke the quiet.

"I'm with you!" Lockjaw said, putting a new candy into his mouth.

"I'll go cuz I don't know anyone who's that lucky with money," I reasoned.

"What if we don't find the other half?"

"As my father always says, just because you have a goal in life doesn't mean you can't get side-tracked for a while." Slick slipped the comb through his hair one more time, making sure he was ready for action. "Look guys, I gotta go."

He rolled up the blind, opened the window and stepped out into the damp winter night. With his black Wellingtons never touching the ground, he glided into the back seat of his powder-blue Caddie which was parked permanently right outside. Slick got the car for free from the garage at the corner. Busted motor. He convinced us to push that thing all the way up the street and then down the lane. We left it outside the window of his bedroom.

In the silence we heard the car door close. It echoed in the night air. We all sat in the dark room as the car radio clicked on with Elvis singing, "Are You Lonesome Tonight". His soft tenor voice drifted in through the open window. A small squeal was heard from Doreen in the back seat.

There was no doubt in any of our minds that night, during the second blizzard of the year, that Slick, at thirteen, was a genius.

"Hey, Dennis." Lockjaw looked up from his bag of jujubes, "you think your sister Nadine would go out with me?"

"No." Dennis thought a bit then he added. "But you could ask her and get turned down."

Harry and Bartholomew

I ENTERED THE WRITING CONTEST on a dare from Nadine, Dennis's sister. It all started in our ninth-grade class in high school. It was late in the school year and the warm early summer sun was blasting in through the large open window. I started out thinking about the job I'd have to get for the summer holidays. I had some options – bagging groceries, life-guarding at the community pool, working with my mother at the hospital where she worked. That was the last thing I wanted to do. Watching sick people being sick depressed me.

The class was dead quiet as Mrs. McCormick, our teacher, read from a book written by someone named James Joyce. I tried my best to listen but my mind wandered back into a dream I had. My dream concerned a poet who was flamboyant. He had a thick black mustache, smoked smelly French cigarettes, and was very popular with the ladies. In my dream, I wrote poetry on big oversized pieces of paper, on walls, ceilings, on people's skin in small print and large. I was considered by everyone to be the last of the really 'Great Poets'.

Every time I would see the poet's face in my dream, his face was mine.

My eyes began to tear up. Nadine, who was sitting behind me, tapped me on the shoulder. I turned and she saw the tears in my eyes. She instantly placed her hand over her open mouth.

"He is great, isn't he?"

I had no idea what or who she was talking about. "What?"

"You are so sensitive." Her hand reached out and brushed a tear from my cheek.

The next day Nadine and I were at the community swimming pool over on Marcel Avenue. She wanted to know why I was crying during the James Joyce reading. So I told her about my poet dream. She greeted the dream with a very sassy smile.

"Why, Ben, you have illusions of grandeur."

"What the hell is that?"

"Well...." She sat and thought for the longest time. "It's kinda like the mayor. He has them."

"The mayor of the city?"

"Uh huh."

"How can you tell?"

"Cuz he thinks, and that's the key word, thinks ... that's he better than anyone else. And my mother says, no one is better than anyone else."

"That's what *my* mother says! And she says it to me all the time!" I reached over and put my hand on Nadine's arm.

She placed her hand on top of mine and gave it a tender squeeze. "It's only a dream, Ben. You don't really have illusions of grandeur. You, Ben, I mean. You don't really have them."

"How can you be sure?"

"Because I've known you all my life and if you had illusions of grandeur, I wouldn't be sitting here."

I looked over at Nadine. Her eyes were big and bright. I could feel her hand on mine gently rubbing the tops of my fingers. I stared. All I could think about was, the mayor of the city had illusions of grandeur! I think it was the first time in my life I'd ever

thought about politicians.

I felt her squeeze my fingers tenderly. "So, can you write something for me?"

Her voice snapped me back to reality. "No…. No, no. I'm not a poet. Really."

"How do you know? Have you ever tried?"

"I've never tried to write anything!"

"This is a sign."

"A sign! What kind a sign?"

"It's a dream sign!" Nadine looked into my eyes, her lips were tight and her smile stretched across her face. "Write me something."

"What? Now?"

"No, not now. When you go home and you're sitting alone at the kitchen table or wherever it is you write your homework."

"What do you want me to write about?"

"Whatever. You decide."

"I wouldn't know where to begin."

"At the beginning, silly." She jumped up off her towel and ran to the side of the pool.

"The beginning of what?"

She looked back over her shoulder and winked. "You and me."

She effortlessly dove into the pool, hardly making any splash at all.

That evening I finished my homework and thought about Nadine. She wanted me to write something about her and me. Now, Nadine and I were not an item. We've known each other since we were nine. We were just friends, we'd never once gone out on a date or held hands or kissed or done anything, really. Sure, we would have a Pepsi and fries together over at the Donut Hole, but that wasn't a date or anything. We were just having some fries together. We didn't drink out of the same glass or anything. So writing something about her and me was kind of hard. I knew she liked ice cream, lipstick, baseball, the colour green, swimming, diving, school, she cried easy at movies and her favourite food was French fries. Other than that, what could I write about? So I decided to write about my cat.

Harry and Bartholomew

Bartholomew was a tall fellow with long black legs and paws. His silky fur was short, soft and very black. In fact, he was all black, not a speck of colour anywhere. His eyes were that golden colour that you see on really beautifully painted tops of Chinese chopsticks.

Bart was not a particularly curious cat. No, he would rather sit right beside you on the chair, the couch, or the bed. He'd go outside and sit on the top of the post looking down his driveway toward the traffic on the street, scrutinizing passers-by.

Every now and then his golden eyes would catch sight of a mouse scampering up the side of the drive. But Bart would hardly have moved at all. He wasn't that interested in catching mice or chasing squirrels. It was too tiring. He thought that everyone had a right to do whatever it was that made them happy.

Bartholomew loved the finer things of life. Petting, loving, being held, kisses, purring really loud and licking the tips of his paws. He really preferred lying back on a soft, warm pillow closing his golden eyes and taking life as it came.

He was lying on the couch drifting off to sleep when he felt something touch his reclining paw. He opened his eyes and there was a brown furry creature staring back at him. It was a small, brown mouse named Harry. Harry lived in the far north-east corner of the kitchen, under the old refrigerator. For years Bart had chased Harry. He'd finally given up because Harry was just too fast. Harry had figured out times of the day when Bartholomew was in the kitchen so he would just peek out at him or tease him and run behind him when Bart wasn't looking. Harry sometimes would just run out, stop in the middle of the kitchen floor, and stare at Bart who was lying on the floor in the doorway. If Bart flicked a muscle, Harry would cock his head to one side and it seemed to Bart that an inviting smile would appear on Harry's face.

Now, here was Harry sitting within inches of Bart's whiskers. Harry seemed to smile. Bart moved but Harry was gone in an instant. Bart jumped up and began to chase, forgetting for a moment that he had given up chasing. Harry darted into the kitchen. Bart followed. As Bart turned the corner, he saw Harry scurry over to the stove. The bottom drawer was open and Harry went in. Bart hopped up and squeezed into the drawer making all kinds of noise climbing over the pots and pans. Harry stopped in front of a fair-sized hole in the wall and looked back. Bart moved quickly but Harry disappeared into the hole. Bart followed.

He followed Harry through all kinds of holes, bolting through the big ones and squeezing through the small until he came to a spot where there was more than one hole. A fork in the road. Bart didn't know which way to turn.

He was a lost cat.

He looked one way, then the other; then he heard noises coming from one of the holes. He rushed toward the noise, down the hole and followed his nose. He fell out the bottom of the hole and landed in water. Rushing water. Well, Bart was one of those cats who never learned to swim. He spent too much time lying in the sun.

The water pushed Bart down a long round tunnel. His paws paddled as fast as they could just to keep his whiskers above water. It seemed like he was doomed. But then he heard a squeaky voice from the dry side of the tunnel. It was Harry standing on a large piece of wood waving his little hands in the air making mouse noises. Bart meowed as loud as he could. Harry jumped off the wood and began to push it toward Bartholomew. Harry used all his mouse strength until the wood was within reach of Bartholomew. Bart scratched his way onto it safely. Bart and Harry sat side by side, catching their breaths. Bart looked down at his new friend and let out a small meow. Harry looked back and squeaked. They were both glad they were there for each other.

A light breeze was coming in through the window. Bartholomew slowly opened his eyes feeling the edge of the curtain brushing the tip of his ear. Had he just had a cat dream? Or, was it reality?

He shook his head furiously, glanced across the wood floor toward the kitchen. There in the doorway sat Harry. He had what seemed to be a grin on this face. He squeaked and winked. Bart licked his paw, wiped his whiskers, and slowly let his head fall back onto the pillow. Gently he closed his golden eyes.

I was very nervous about what I'd written, and Nadine had been bugging me about finishing it. I wanted to test it out first before I gave it to her, so I asked my mother to take a look at it.

"You've written a story? Lovely!"

I borrowed a tape recorder from a friend and set it up on the kitchen table. I threaded the tape through the recording heads and placed the pages in front of her.

"What are you going to do with that?"

"It's just in case."

"Just in case of what?"

"It's nothing. It's just in case I want to hear it back and change some stuff later on." I tried my best to reason with her and put her mind a rest. "Go ahead. Please." I pushed the record button.

I'm not sure what I felt as I listened to my mother read the story into the microphone, the large reels turning slowly, recording her every word. She read easily, without a misstep. Her voice was strong and clear. She read with so much enjoyment that I began to giggle. Then, after she finished, she placed her warm hand on my cheek and smiled at me.

"Good job," she said as she placed the last page down on the table. "Keep it up."

"You think so?"

"Yes. Yes, I do. It won't win the Pulitzer. But that's okay."

I sat in the kitchen alone, staring at the recorder. I hit the rewind button and when I got back to the beginning of the tape, I pushed 'play'. My mother's voice was clear and perfect. But there was something about it I did not recognize. It had an accent. It had a British accent. At first I didn't know it was my mother. It was the first time in my life that I realized that my mother had an accent. I'd never heard it before. My mother was a foreigner. I knew she was from England, but I just assumed she spoke like me. I was in shock.

Nadine and I met in Trenholm Park the next afternoon. She was sitting beside me on the grass, her back against one of those big oak trees, her arms wrapped tightly around her legs with her chin resting on her knees.

"Did you know my mother has an accent?"

"Of course." She looked up at me. "She's from England."

"I never knew my mother spoke with an accent."

"Are you nuts?"

I just shook my head.

"Come on, read. I'm dying to hear it."

I placed the pages on my lap and began. Nadine was silent the whole time

I was reading the story. I glanced over every now and then to see if she had fallen asleep. She hadn't. She just sat there grinning up at me. When I finished she reached over and gently took the pages from my hand. "Well, Ben you are a poet."

"Well, I don't know."

She got up, went over and leaned against the park bench. She looked over at me sitting against the tree.

"So, am I the cat or the mouse?"

"I guess it depends on how fast you can run." I smiled.

"Well, you know that I know how to swim."

I slapped my leg and began to laugh out loud.

She joined my laughter with a chuckle. She stopped, cocked her head over to one side and looked straight into my eyes with that sassy smile of hers. "So, let the chase begin."

I went silent.

The Damp Latin at The Grand

SLICK WAS WAITING FOR ME at the Donut Hole. It was up on Sherbrooke Street. The Donut Hole had the best fries in the neighbourhood. Way better than Ben's Deluxe or Dunn's Famous. And they always gave you a big plate full.

I could live on fries and a Pepsi. Everybody knew that fries and a burger were my favourite meal.

Slick was dressed in his usual Wellingtons, jeans and white tee-shirt. His boot was resting on the seat of his favourite booth with his usual glass of root beer – nasty stuff. He was waiting anxiously to hear my report on my date with Maria Delano. I had been very nervous. I parked myself down across from him. I waved at Betty, the waitress, and yelled, "Could I get fries and a Pepsi?"

We had met at the Donut Hole a few days earlier when he had convinced me that the Maria Delano date was something I had to do and that I was ready for it. Considering his vast experience, I listened as he gave me a serious checklist, reams of advice for me to memorize for the momentous occasion. Slick had already spent hours feeling girls up in the back seat of his old '44 Caddie out back of his place. This was going to be the first time in my thirteen years of life I was going to touch a girl's breast. At least, I was hoping to. And that breast I was prepping for, the one that

belonged to Maria Delano, made the occasion beyond my wildest dreams.

"So what's the news? How'd it go?" His voice was calm and casual.

"Do I have to tell ya?"

"Well, that was the deal. I told you what to do and you tell me what happened."

"Shit, it's embarrassing."

"It won't be the last time. At least, that's what they say."

Betty, our waitress, put a Pepsi on the table.

"Fries are on the way," she said as she quickly passed by.

When she was out of earshot, I turned to Slick who was grinning from ear to ear.

"Okay, okay. We went to the movies over at The Grand. I even took a shower just to make sure I smelled right. We sat at the back. We touched shoulders. Her breathing was heavy. I felt lucky. This would be my night."

"You're writing again, Ben. Get to the point." He sipped hard on his root beer.

"Can't help it."

"Okay, never mind. Write. … Write, but write faster."

"I turned my head and watched her watching the movie. My God, she was beautiful! I turned my head back to the screen. A couple of seconds passed and then I felt it, her leg against the side of my leg. There we sat shoulders and legs touching for the longest time. I felt her head turn, her eyes on me, those dark, brown eyes burning into me. I wanted to turn and look, but I couldn't. I kept my head still and moved my eyes as far as they would go toward her. It got to the point where I thought my eyes would turn right around in their sockets. She turned her head quickly back to the screen. I was desperate! Desperate to kiss her! I turned to her once more. The light from the screen gave her face an angelic look. Her face seemed to shine in the light."

"Shit, you're driving me crazy!" Slick leaned back on his seat grabbing a fist full of his thick, black hair.

"I leaned in a little closer to kiss her cheek. She turned her face toward mine, kissed me full on the lips! And then put her tongue in my mouth! I was in shock. We both simultaneously snapped our heads back to the screen."

"My God, the 'Damp Latin' put her tongue in your mouth! Oh, this is good!" Slick said, shaking his head.

"At first I thought it was disgusting but that went away real quick. So, I did what you said and I went into action right away. I put my arm around her and rested my hand on her far shoulder. Slowly I began to move my hand down her shoulder to her breast."

"Not too quick now!" Slick pointed at me.

"No. … No, I was calm! When my hand was full on her breast, she placed her hand on mine. It felt a bit damp but I expected that, she is, after all, Maria Delano, the Damp Latin. Without ever taking my eyes off the screen, I slowly moved my other hand to her knee and began to inch my way to the mound of…."

I couldn't get the word out of my mouth, which was dry, so I took a sip of my Pepsi.

"Venus, Venus. How many times do I have to tell you?" He slurped up the root beer through the straw.

"Right, right. Her naked thigh was wet and sticky, but she was, as I said, Maria Delano the damp Latin."

"And you were in love! I get it!" Slick took another sip of root beer.

"Yeah, I was in love! I felt her head rest firmly on my shoulder and her wet hand rest firmly on my chest. As my hand made its way up her naked wet thigh, her hand worked its way up my chest to my face. I was excited beyond belief! We were both breathing hard and loud. I couldn't hear the movie anymore. All I could make out was the sound of Maria breathing heavy on my shoulder. Now even my shoulder was getting wet from her hot breath. Her sticky fingers came to rest on my lips!"

Betty put down my fries.

"Thanks."

"Pas de problem, Romeo," she answered back in French.

I reached for the vinegar. Slick raised his hand to stop me so he could say something, but I was on a roll and couldn't stop.

"My hand had almost reached the often talked about 'land of pleasure.' I was closing in on sheer ecstasy."

Slick slowly picked up a fry and popped it in his mouth.

"My hand that was on her shoulder was now resting on her perfect right breast. It was perfect!"

"Got ya. It was perfect." Slick grabbed another fry.

"No, I mean it was perfectly round. I'd never felt anything so perfectly round. It was like a softball but squishier."

"You're with the Damp Latin and you're thinking baseball!"

"That's when I realized that my other hand wasn't on her naked thigh at all. See, Maria was munching on a bag of chocolate covered raisins and my hand was in that open bag of chocolate-covered raisinets that was resting between her steamy thighs!"

"Oh, my God!" Slick popped another fry.

"Yeah, that guardian of the mound of Venus had melted and my hand was buried in a sea of chocolate covered floating raisins. Her fingers on the edge of my mouth tasted of chocolate. The tips of my fingers that were resting on her breast were wet and sticky. When the movie was finished and we went outside into the daylight, I found we were both covered in milk chocolate. Everywhere Maria's hands went there was chocolate. Everywhere my hands went there was chocolate!"

"So, did she say anything while you were feeling her breast?"

"Not a word. She squirmed a bit but neither of us said anything. I was afraid if I said anything, she would see that it was me feeling her up and hit me."

"So what was so embarrassing?"

"I was covered in chocolate! My mother freaked out!"

"Did ya tell her how ya got the chocolate on ya?"

"Hell, no!"

"So what are you gonna do now?" Slick asked, sucking up the last of his root beer.

"Well, I've already seen the movie."

"Right. You wanna use the back of the Caddie?"

"You'd let me use it?"

"Sure."

"Really!"

"Yeah. So long as I can watch."

"No way. It's tough enough getting my arm around her in the first place but if you're watching then it could take me all night."

"Okay, okay. The Caddie's yours. But ya gotta promise to tell me everything. And I mean everything! Okay?" Slick grabbed another fry off my plate.

"You want another fries?" Betty said, coming over to the table.

I looked down at my plate. It was empty. I looked up at Slick.

"Sorry, Ben. Just couldn't stop eatin' those damn things."

"No thanks, Betty. I'm not that hungry any more."

She shrugged her shoulders and walked away. I looked back at Slick.

"That's okay. I'll tell you one thing, even though Maria Delano is the Damp Latin, her breasts kept me up all night last night."

"What? Dreamin' of baseball?" He laughed.

"No." I put my two hands on my chest. "You know!"

"Wahoo!" Slick's voice echoed throughout the Donut Hole.

I reached over and put my hand on Slick's shoulder and to my surprise it felt very much like Maria's breast, a baseball but mushier. My mind slipped back to The Grand Cinema and my hand, in the dark, sliding across Maria's back in my quest to touch something soft.

Then a flash came to me of Maria and me, sitting in the back of Slick's Caddie, the neighbourhood shrine. It might be as unforgettable as the first time I remembered stepping into St. Joseph's Oratory up on Queen Mary Road, but with a lot more heavy breathing.

No Place Like Home

I WAS HEADING HOME from the Montreal Poolroom where I had a steamie and fries with the gang. It was one of our favourite new spots on The Main. They had the best dogs in town. I was carrying an old small train set in a shopping bag that Dennis had given me. He told me it still worked and I mentioned to him I had a place to take it. I was excited that Easter was just a few days away. It always seemed to give me hope that spring was right around the corner.

It had been raining all day. It was a cold, heavy rain along with a cool wind coming from the north, the normal Montreal April weather. As I rounded the corner, the flashing red lights of an ambulance from Saint John's Hospital flickered off the wet pavement. Someone in white pants and a raincoat was opening the back doors and a stretcher was pulled out. It was wheeled toward the laneway by two other burley fellows, also dressed in white.

A small crowd had gathered, mumbling nothings to each other. I approached the crowd. Mr. Delano, Maria's dad, was there, looking very concerned.

"What happened?" I asked.

"Taking her away." Mr. Delano responded with the finality of a doctor who was telling you that you only had 24 hours to live.

"Who?

"Mrs. Curran," he said.

"Old Lady Beer?" I said, listening intently.

"Yea," he responded knowingly. "I think that's what this is all about," he confided. "They found her in the alley."

"Is she dead?"

"Don't think so. Just asleep."

Suddenly we heard a scream coming from the laneway.

"Well, she's not going peacefully," Mr. Delano said, clapping his hands together.

"I always thought she was a nice woman. At least she was always nice to me."

Mr. Delano looked over at me and with that fed up look I've seen before and said, "You…. I always thought you were a bit of an idiot, Ben."

The sound of the stretcher being pushed through the alley got the crowd into a bit of a frenzy. Everyone pushed forward to see her. Her head was shaking from side to side. Her arms and legs were strapped in along the sides of the stretcher. There was something sad about this. Old Lady Beer.

"Is she drooling?" asked Mr. Delano.

"Is she what?" I shot back.

"She's drooling?" Mrs. Novak joined the conversation.

Mrs. Novak was from Finland and she carried all the physical characteristics – blonde hair, blue eyes, very stately, and she always looked really, really clean.

"No, he asked 'if' she was drooling." I smiled at her. She was not an unattractive woman.

"It's usually one of the signs," Mr. Delano confided to Mrs. Novak.

"I know. It's so embarrassing," she responded with sorrow.

Over at the back doors of the ambulance, the man in white on

the far side of the stretcher whispered, "Which end goes in first?"

He must have been the rookie.

"Just grab that side," the other man in white said. And with a quick lift and a push, the stretcher began to disappear into the dark of the inside of the ambulance. I caught a glimpse of the face on the stretcher.

A hand gripped my arm. It belonged to Mr. Delano. "It's her husband!" he said, with complete disbelief. He then motioned with his head back over his shoulder.

I went over and looked down the alley and 'Old Lady Beer' was still there lying on the back stairs leading up to her house.

"Hide the liquor!" Mr. Curran screamed from inside the ambulance as it was pulling away. "I can't take it anymore! I can't take it anymore!"

The sound of his voice made the hair on my arms stand up. I could feel them through my damp, musky-smelling wool coat. His voice was shrill and desperate. I watched as the ambulance, with its sirens blearing, disappeared down the street. I finally turned and headed toward my front door.

As I walked into the house, the smell of tourtière filled the air. My mother and my sister, Winn, sat at the table arguing. They seemed to be at the point where neither of them knew what the argument was about anymore. Nothing they were saying made any sense to me.

"Hey, you guys see what happened outside with Old Lady Beer?" I said putting my bag down by the door. "Well, did ya?" But they weren't listening.

"It's not your life!" Winn said in that rebellious tone of hers.

"I know," my mother shot back. She added as an afterthought, "Thank God!"

My mother spoke a lot in afterthoughts. She was really good at it. First, she'd agree with you and then she'd tell you what she really thought. And with that thought came 'the look'. Her blue eyes would shimmer with sarcasm. It was an art she'd mastered. Most of the time it was real funny. But every now and then she'd hit you with a zinger and life wasn't funny anymore.

"What've you got in the bag?" Winn asked trying to avoid the zinger.

"Train set," I replied, sitting down.

"You want something to eat?" my mother snapped.

"Yeah, sure,"

"It's in the oven," she stated.

"Great." I answered back, not moving.

My mother got up in a huff and moved to the stove.

"I'm too old for a train set." Winn stared at me.

"Forget it, will ya?"

"What? You got some kids out there we don't know about?" There was mischief in her voice.

"My God, he's fourteen years old! Winn, sometimes you say the damnedest things," my mother said, bringing a slice of tourtière over and placing it in front of me.

"Here!" she said, handing me a fork.

"Well, you're never too young. That's what they say," Winn laughed. "Who the hell is the train set for? Or do I have to kill ya!" Winn was a very persistent person once she got her teeth into something.

"It's for a kid. Any ketchup?"

"Yes," my mother said, getting up from the table and moving to the fridge.

"Well?" Winn said pointing to the shopping bag on the floor.

"Alright. Look, I got it from Dennis. He got it when he was a kid and didn't want it anymore."

"Yeaaaah ... sooo?" She dragged out the words in one long breath.

I looked down at the steaming tourtière on the plate in front of me. "I'm taking it over to the community centre toy pile."

"Why Ben! You're on the road to being a nice, thoughtful guy," she said as if she really meant it.

"But every now and then he gets off the bus," my mother added tapping me on the back of the head. She placed the ketchup in front of me. "At least he's got brains enough to get a transfer," she fired the zinger at Winn.

"Where is everybody?" I asked, trying to put out the fire.

"Your other sister, Beth, Winn ... somebody help!" My mother said snapping her fingers.

"Maggie?" I jumped in.

"Yeah, she's at church helping with the flowers."

"And Frankie's in the bathroom," Winn added.

"I didn't see him go in," I reasoned.

"You didn't. Went in there over an hour ago."

"Wow! An hour? What is that, a record?"

"Yup!" Winn said, as if it was nothing out of the ordinary.

"What's he doing in there?"

"Well, he's not combing his hair!" my mother shot back. "He's losing that!" That zinger fell on deaf ears. "Some milk?" she asked with a touch on my arm.

"That'd be great, Mum," I responded, shoving a piece of tourtière into my mouth. I picked up the ketchup and poured some over my pie. "Who's putting water in the ketchup?"

"Not me." Winn looked over at my mother.

"Well, it goes further that way." She glared at Winn.

Winn put down her teacup and leaned across the table. Her voice had that hushed quality to it. This was something she really didn't want our mother to hear.

"I met this doctor the other night down at The Dominion. Well, he's not actually a full doctor – like he can't operate on you or anything like that. But he's in his third year at McGill and he's cute as hell." She smiled up at me with those 'Curious George' eyes. "Okay, okay," she waved her hand at me encouraging me closer. She cupped her hand on the side of her mouth hiding her lips from my mother. "He's taking psychology which has something to do with your brains!"

"Okay," I said, trying to follow her and at the same time giving her every indication that I was.

"He says that he could delve into people's brains and figure out their problems. It's not that tough, he says. Like Elvis and that jiggling he does, or Einstein and his brain.

"He figured out Einstein?"

"Yeah!"

"While you were sitting there?"

"Oh yeah! I told him about Old Lady Beer, right? He said it definitely has something to do with her father."

"What does?"

"The drinking! The beer thing."

"It has something to do with her father?" I asked, chewing on a piece of tourtière.

"It's a substitute for her father. The pain her father went through in life. The pain she put her father through in life. Or the pain she feels because she loves her father too much," she said, without taking a breath.

"The crust is a little dry this year, Mum," I offered.

"I don't know what the hell it is about college guys," Winn chuckled.

"Or sailors, teachers, shoemakers, coalminers, salesmen, circus clowns," my mother said returning with my glass of milk in her hand. "Should I go on?" she added, her eyes locked onto Winn.

Winn threw her hands in the air and smiled over at me. "That's just pure sarcasm, Mum. But I'm accepting nothing but gifts this Easter," Winn answered without malice.

"Well, I don't know anything about Old Lady Beer's father but it was Mr. Curran they had strapped to the stretcher," I said.

"What?"

My mother stood in front of the bathroom door and then yelled another name, "Robert ... Ben ... Will! Oh, God!" She turned to Winn. "Who the hell's in there?"

"Frankie," Winn answered back.

"Frankie!" My mother always had trouble with our names. "If you don't come out here right now, I'm going to break down this door! Frankie! Do you hear me?" Mum started banging on the bathroom door.

"Hey, now I know where you get that 'banging on the door' thing." I looked at Winn.

She ignored me. "They took her husband, eh?"

"Yeah! That's who they had on the stretcher."

"Mr. Curran? They took Mr. Curran?" Winn said in disbelief.

"Yeah, Mr. Curran, they took him instead of her. Maybe it's got something to do with his father."

"Oh, very funny, Ben." My sister sat back in her chair. "What did they do with her?"

"Left her asleep on the steps in the alley."

"Frankie, you're going to kill yourself, mark my words!" Mum kneeled down, peeked in the keyhole of the door and whispered, "Are you asleep in there?"

"I don't get it," Winn said.

"He's asleep in there," my mother informed us all.

"But, Mr. Curran's not crazy!" Winn said after a moment's thought.

"Of course he's crazy. How could he not be? Staying with that woman for twenty-two years," my mother interjected. "Oh, and by the way, her father's dead! Been dead for years," she looked toward Winn. "There's only one person to blame in this world for any of the stuff that happens to you and that person is yourself! So, the next time you meet up with someone that believes that whatever you do is someone else's fault, I hope you've got the brains, and enough sense in you, to run away from them as fast as you can," she said with authority.

I picked up the glass of milk and downed it. My sister watched me as I drank and when I'd finished the entire glass, she looked down at my plate. "That dry, huh?"

"Don't you start," Mum cautioned her.

"I told you. More lard. You gotta put in more lard," Winn argued.

"And I'm telling you, don't start."

"When we were kids you used a lot more lard."

"Yeah," I agreed. "Isn't that what holds this stuff together?" I asked, pointing at the crust on my plate.

The door of the bathroom slowly opened. Frankie stuck his head around the open door. He still had his hat on, one of those Sinatra fedoras.

"Shit, it's hot in 'ere!" he said, wiping his brow with the sleeve of his overcoat. He stumbled over to the table. He opened his eyes really wide. "Whoaaaaa'!"

"You didn't take off your coat and hat before you went in there?" I asked.

"I don't 'member goin' in there. Did somebody tell me to go in there?"

"No. But whatever you do, don't blame it on your father," Winn cautioned.

"I'm glad you've taken some good advice." My mother smiled at my sister.

"Boy, what a day!" Frankie piped up.

"The office was nuts! Everybody wanted whatever it was they wanted right away! I don't think I ate! The drink I had at noon … oh boy!" He tried to take his coat off but his arm kept catching in his sleeve and he starting spinning around on the spot, mumbling to himself. "Last thing I 'member I was on stage at the Flamingo singing 'As Time Goes By' and next thing Mum's pounding on the bathroom door."

"You'll get over it. Some pie?" Mum held up the tourtière in the pie plate.

"No," he moaned, grabbing his stomach.

I looked at my brother trying to figure out if he was drunk or if he was about to be sick. He didn't look good. Sweat poured down his forehead.

"Take your coat off, sit down and stay for awhile."

"I'm tryin'!"

Mum returned the pie to the oven. "You look like you've been hit by a bus. Are you drunk? I've told you hundreds of times…."

'Noooooooooo." Frankie cut her off with the longest no in the world and finally got his arm out of his sleeve and plunked himself down at the table with Winn and me.

"I'm just warning you. Alright, I'm going to take a little lie-down," my mother announced as she started to leave the kitchen. She stopped at the door. "This evening's Easter Mass. Promise me you'll all be there. Maggie's doing the flowers." We all agreed reluctantly and she headed down the hallway to her bedroom.

I looked back at my sister and brother. "Are you going?"

"I'd better," Winn reasoned, "or she might hold back on my Easter gift. And I sure could use the underwear."

"You already know what she's giving you?" I questioned her.

"Of course! Want to know what you're getting?"

"I hope I get chocolate Easter eggs!"

"You won't."

"Well, don't tell me!" I warned her.
"What's the fun of not knowing?"
"The surprise?" I said, trying to give her a clue.
"Ah, what kind of surprise? The real surprise or the surprised surprise?"
"What the hell are you talking about?"
"Look, ya bozo, when you open your gift you're genuinely surprised, right? But when I open mine, I already know what it is and I'm still surprised. Surprising?" she said, making herself perfectly clear.
I took a long look at Winn. "You're not quite all there, are ya?"
"Was somebody talking about brains while I was in the bathroom?" Frankie broke his silence.
"Winn. She met some doctor…."
"Whose brains?"
"Mr. Curran's." She rolled her eyes.
"Not mine?"
"No," Winn said. "Mum says you don't have any."
"Ha," he said, trying to laugh it off.
I looked over at Frankie. "So, you hitting the Flamingo again tonight?"
He said nothing. He just stared down at what was left of the tourtière on my plate.
"Dry?" he finally uttered.
"Like a desert!" I reported.
"Ah. What's in the bag?"
"Never mind that!" Winn interrupted. "You hear they took Mr. Curran tonight?"
"What!" Frankie said wiping his forehead again. "No way!"
"Yeah, Ben says they took him." Winn made a circle with her finger on the side of her temple. "Happy Birfday!"
"They didn't take the drinker?"

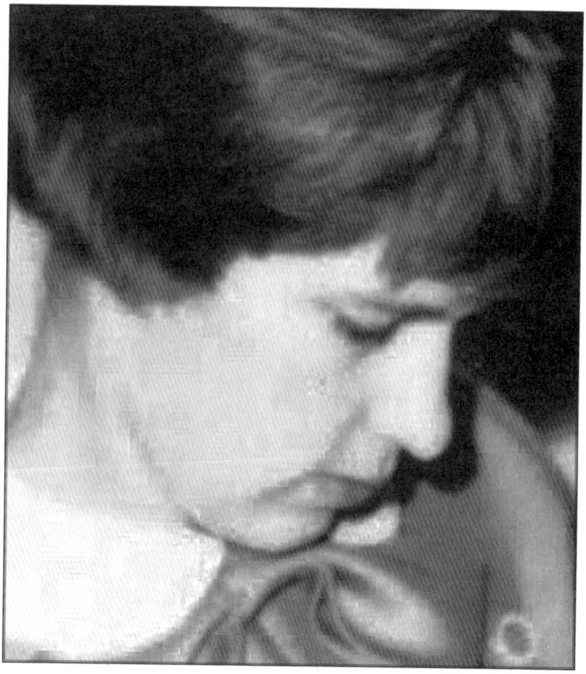

"No. They left her conked out in the alley," Winn informed him.

"They took him on the stretcher and he was screaming like a crazy man all the they down the street," I added.

"Holy cow!"

Maggie waltzed into the kitchen carrying a huge bunch of flowers. My mother was right behind her.

"Where in hell did you get those?" Winn smiled at my sister.

"The church."

"My God, you stole flowers from the church?" My mother covered her mouth with her hand.

"Thought you went to lie down." Frankie rested his hat on the table.

"No. I think you should go lie down!"

"What happened to the palms?" Winn asked Maggie sarcastically.

"That was last week! But how would you know? You weren't there!" My mother shot a look at Winn.

"These were everywhere. It was looking like a funeral instead of Easter Mass."

"So, you had to steal them?" My mother was insistent.

"No! They gave them to me. I thought you'd like them."

"Why, thank you Maggs. Very thoughtful." Her tone changed and she turned to Winn. "You see how thoughtful a daughter can be?"

Winn looked at Frankie and shrugged her shoulders. "Never get a break."

"Think I'll go change if I'm forced to go to church tonight." I got up and started for the kitchen door.

"Hey Maggs, you hear the nut house took Mr. Curran tonight?" Frankie looked up at my sister.

"No!" She passed the flowers to my Mum.

"Yeah, Ben saw him strapped on the stretcher."

"It can't be true. He's not nuts!"

"Winn says it has something to do with his brains!" Frankie took a deep breath.

I stopped in the doorway, picked up my bag and looked back at my family. I felt a sense of relief that I wasn't Mr. Curran on the stretcher, or the kid that never gets chocolate Easter eggs or gifts at Christmas, or the kid that has no family.

Winn looked up at me and smiled. "So, Ben, you sure you don't want to know what you gettin' for Easter?"

I thought for a second and then shook my head." Naw, I like the surprise."

I turned and walked away.

Acknowledgements

There are many who have contributed to this book. I owe great thanks to Wendy O'Brien, who helped edit my writing and without whose encouragement and support you would not be reading these pages. Thanks also to Aprile Royal, Jim Royal, Deborah Burgess, Mike Kirby, Jim Blankenship and many other friends who have supported me in this effort. Of course, my wife, Suzanne, my son, Christopher, and my family of origin who inspired many of these stories – they form the ground of being and are beyond thanks.